Shelley's Acre
Ruth Kirtley

Scripture Union

By the same author
Lion Hunt

Copyright © Ruth Kirtley 2002
First published 2002

Scripture Union, 207–209 Queensway, Bletchley,
Milton Keynes, MK2 2EB, England.
Email: info@scriptureunion.org.uk
Website: www.scriptureunion.org.uk

ISBN 1 85999 602 7

British Library Cataloguing-in-Publication Data.
A catalogue record of this book is available from the British
Library.

Printed and bound in Great Britain by Creative Print and
Design (Wales) Ebbw Vale.

Scripture Union is an international Christian charity working
with churches in more than 130 countries, providing
resources to bring the good news about Jesus Christ to
children, young people and families and to encourage them
to develop spiritually through the Bible and prayer.

As well as our network of volunteers, staff and associates
who run holidays, church-based events and school Christian
groups, we produce a wide range of publications and
support those who use our resources through training
programmes.

For Katie Davies, who encouraged me.

Chapter One

Maybe I'm invisible?

Matt sat at the kitchen table one evening in spring, spearing chips with his fork. Conversations bounced to and fro across him till he felt like the umpire at a crazy tennis match.

"She said your appointment was 4.30 *today*." Mum was giving Dad a phone message.

"...but then they found that the rabbit had chewed right through the cable!" Dad was telling Mum a funny story he'd heard on the train home that evening.

"I can... *mph*... sell my bike... *glup*... 'n then I'll have enough to... *slurp*... buy it." Harry, the oldest, with hair dyed in brown and blonde tufts, was shovelling chips like it was a How-much-can-you-eat-in-three-minutes? challenge and telling Stuart about the new guitar he wanted.

"Uh-huh... mm." Stuart, the middle one, was reading a computer magazine and grunting at Harry.

No one was speaking to Matt. They seemed to have forgotten he was there. He sighed.

Yup, definitely invisible.

When you're the youngest and the quietest in a noisy family it sometimes feels as though no one can see you. Mostly Matt didn't mind because he knew Mum and Dad loved him and even Harry and Stuart sort of liked him... most of the time. Everyone was busy, though; going to work and college, talking on the phone, dashing off to things in the evening, and sometimes there was just so much noise. Mainly it was Harry practising his electric guitar and arguing with Mum and Dad about everything, or Stuart explaining complicated science experiments to anyone who'd listen or playing very loud music while he did his homework. Just sometimes Matt wished everyone would be quiet and listen to *him* for a change.

"More chips, anyone?" Mum pointed to the dish. Harry stopped shovelling and held out his plate. Dad started asking Stuart how his physics test had gone.

"There's a new boy in my class," Matt said into a little quiet gap. Mum heard.

"Is there, love; what's his name?"

"Ellis. He lives in one of the new houses by Shelley's Farm."

"Oh, Rickyard Close; where the old farmyard used to be?" said Dad. Matt nodded.

"I love the way they've done up the old barn and stables," said Mum. "It was a shame to see those beautiful old buildings slowly falling down. I'm not so keen on the new houses they've built beside them, though."

"Huh, anyone who lives there'll be unpopular," grunted Stuart, not looking up from his magazine. "Using good farmland for more houses!"

"Nico says they'll bring more business for us at Planet Pizza." Harry gulped down his last chip and joined the new conversation.

"Do you imagine they're going to live on nothing

but takeaway pizzas?" Stuart asked scornfully.

"Well, I could do with a few more shifts, if I'm going to buy that guitar," said Harry.

Hey, this was my conversation! How come other people always take over?

"People have got to live somewhere," said Dad.

"Yes, but not *here*," said Stuart. "If they build on all our countryside it'll spoil the ecological balance in our environment and change the character of the town. More people means more cars, more roads, an increase in pollution levels..."

"Yawn-yawn!" groaned Harry. "Time for another lecture from Professor Boff-Brain!"

"Give it a rest, you two," Dad laughed. "Those new houses have certainly stirred up feelings in the town. We've got one half saying that the town's going to be ruined for ever and the other half saying 'Hooray for Progress!' Not sure which half I belong to yet."

"Well, I know that it makes me sad to see the old farmhouse surrounded by those new houses," sighed Mum. "I can remember when it was all still fields on both sides of this road. Grannie used to take me up to the yard there to see the ducks when I was very small."

"But places keep changing," said Harry. "Remember that amazingly brilliant history project I did when I was at school? This town wasn't here in Roman times; there was just a couple of villas with farms along this road, because it was like this important motorway to the sea!"

"Mm, that's right," said Mum. "I'd just started working at the library and I got you some local history information, didn't I?"

"Yeah, two hundred years ago; it was just this titchy village with a lot of fields full of sheep and things." Harry was getting enthusiastic now. "The biggest field was the Shire Lea and that got changed to Shirley and then Shelley…"

"Who's giving the lecture now?" Stuart muttered.

"Shh, Stuart, this is interesting," said Dad. "It's amazing how the town has grown over the years, and we can't really complain too much, because what would have happened if people had stopped *our* house being built, back in the 1960s?"

"All right," said Stuart. "So we need to build new houses, but we should be more careful about *where* we build them. We need to think about how the things we do might affect our environment."

"I agree with you, Stuart," said Mum. "But it still doesn't change the fact that the new houses are in the yard and people are starting to move in; we can't blame *them* for what's happened."

"How long has Ellis' family been here?" asked Dad.

"They moved in on Saturday," Matt replied. "The house wasn't ready in the holidays, that's why he's only just started at school."

"Poor thing," said Mum. "It's tough starting a new school and even worse when the term's already begun. What's he like?"

"Dunno really," Matt shrugged. "Jem and me sat with him at lunch time and then we walked home with him after school."

"That was kind," said Mum. "I expect he'll be feeling a bit lonely." Matt wasn't sure about that.

Mrs Brown, their form tutor, had introduced Ellis at registration and Matt and Jem, who was really

Jemima, had tried to talk to him at lunch time. Jem was always friendly to everyone and she just went up to Ellis and started chatting. Matt wanted to be friendly too, but the trouble was that Ellis didn't seem to want to talk. He was polite, but he answered all their questions abruptly, using hardly any words. His eyes were looking far away, as if his body was sitting there in the canteen but his mind was somewhere else. After school it had been the same. Ellis didn't seem to mind them walking with him, but he might as well have been on his own because he took no notice of them.

Then, at the turning into Rickyard Close he'd muttered, "Live here. Bye," and walked off down the new pavement to the first house. It stood in its plot of raw earth, all brand-new bricks and shiny windows, with a pile of turfs by the garage, like brown and green swiss rolls, waiting to be laid.

Matt shrugged. "Maybe he is lonely, but he doesn't seem very interested in being friends," he said.

"Perhaps he's shy," Mum suggested. "Don't give up on him too soon, eh?"

Matt nodded and finished off his chips while Harry and Stuart began to argue about whose turn it was to help with the dishes.

"I've got three tests next week; I need to revise," said Stuart, unbending his tall, skinny body and picking up his magazine.

"So? I'm working till ten tonight; I need to rest!" Harry's hair seemed to get spikier, to match his mood.

"Look, if this is a busy competition, I think Dad or I might win!" said Mum. "I did a long shift at the library today *and* I've cooked tea. Dad's had to travel to work and back on that horrible train and he's got to go out again to a church meeting tonight. We're *all* busy; that's why we take turns, so get a move on and sort it out!"

Dad disappeared upstairs and Stuart and Harry went to the kitchen, still arguing. Suddenly the room was quiet. Mum smiled at Matt.

"Phew; that's better! Are you going to Club tonight?" Matt nodded. He liked Club. He'd looked forward to going for ages but, now he was in Year 7, he was able to go at last. Club was at the church he went to with his family. You could play things like snooker and table tennis and every week there was a special activity as well, like 5-a-side football or a treasure hunt. Baz and Steffi were in charge and they were good fun. They weren't as old as Mum and Dad but they weren't as young as Harry and Stuart. Baz was fantastic at football and Steffi wore really cool clothes. Matt knew loads of people there, from school and from the group he was in on Sunday mornings, and they had a good time. He and Jem went together because they lived very near each other.

"Am I taking you tonight?" asked Mum.

"No, Jem's mum," Matt replied. 'I'm going round her house just before seven."

"So you've got time for some homework before you go," said Mum. Matt pulled a face. "Or would you rather join the other two in the kitchen?"

Hm, a hard choice. It only took a second to decide; Matt hurried upstairs.

Chapter Two

The next morning Matt and Jem walked together to school. They took their usual short cut, crossing the main road where they lived and following the footpath across the grassy field opposite. This was Shelley's Acre, though it measured much more than an acre, or a hectare, as Stuart the Boff-brain often reminded people. He was really fussy about details like that. The land belonged to Shelley's Farm. In the past it had been used for grazing cattle but now it was empty and, ever since Matt could remember, the farmer had never used it. He mowed the grass for hay and kept the footpath clear but nothing else. Once you got away from the road and traffic noises, you could imagine you were out in the country somewhere, instead of on the edge of a town.

Years ago someone had made a really good bike track in a corner near the back. Matt and his friends used it and, because there were houses overlooking, it was safe for them to go there alone. Lots of people used the footpath to cut the corner. It crossed the field, went through the old churchyard, around the little old church and came out on the road that passed the school.

"Did you do that science homework?" asked Jem.

"Stuart helped me," Matt replied.

"You're lucky to have such a brainy brother," Jem sighed, shrugging her school bag along her shoulder. "Mum didn't have a clue!" She didn't seem very worried, but then, nothing seemed to get her down for long.

Matt had known Jem since primary school and they were good friends. She was bright and cheerful, like a sunny day. She and her mum lived three houses down from Matt in a house full of colourful and interesting things, mostly made by Jem's mum, who taught art and design at the college nearby. Matt liked the way that even ordinary things like chairs or shelves could look special in Jem's house. There were unusual pictures on the walls and cushions and curtains in amazing patterns. Jem even managed to look different in her school uniform. Today her shoelaces were bright pink and she had a yellow felt sunflower stuck to her school bag.

They opened the gate and walked through the churchyard. The grass had been cut recently and the old, crooked gravestones looked as though they were poking through torn slits in a piece of green carpet. The church was very old and it was built of red bricks and pieces of knobbly grey flint. It had an orange tiled roof that sagged a bit in the middle and a little bell tower. It sat comfortably in the grass, low and dumpy, like a sleeping tortoise.

"Stuart reckons the people in Rickyard Close will be unpopular," said Matt.

"Why?"

"Well, their houses are built on the old farm and they spoil the countryside," said Matt, remembering what Stuart had said.

"But it's not their fault. They didn't build the houses," Jem pointed out. "There's Ellis," she added. They had walked out of the churchyard and on to the main road, just as Ellis turned out of Rickyard Close ahead of them.

"Hey! New Kid!" Joey, Tim and Dawn pushed past them and ran to catch up with Ellis.

"Uh-oh, it's The Mouth!" muttered Matt, slowing down. Joey was in their year at school. He was loud and tough and he and his mates, people like Tim and Dawn, were Premier League troublemakers. Most people kept out of their way as much as they could; it was safer to do that. Matt and Jem watched as Joey and the others crowded round Ellis.

"Hey, New Kid, I'm talking to you!" said Joey, loudly. "Might interest you to know, my dad's out of work 'cause of you! Yeah, him and some others, they used to work on Shelley's Farm. Farmer sells up, no land to work on, just lots of smart new houses. How does that make you feel, huh?" Ellis walked on, ignoring him. "You deaf or what?" Joey shouted. He didn't like being ignored. Matt was worried.

Ellis is in trouble! Joey can make life bad for people he doesn't like. Now would be a really good time to be invisible... but maybe I should help Ellis.

"Hi, Ellis!" Jem had hurried forward to join him. She smiled at Joey and the others. "'Scuse me, I need to talk to Ellis, OK?" Matt caught them up and watched Joey nervously. Joey didn't know what to do so he just walked off, muttering, with

Tim and Dawn following.

"Phew! Nice one, Jem," said Matt.

She's brave! Wish it'd been me who rescued Ellis.

"Me and Matt are going over the Acre after school," said Jem. "Want to come?"

"Where?"

"Shelley's Acre," Jem explained. "It's a field near here."

"You'll need a bike. Have you got one?" asked Matt. He was still feeling embarrassed about not helping Ellis out, so he wanted to show he was friendly, too.

"Yes," Ellis grunted as he plodded down the road.

He doesn't say much, does he? Maybe he doesn't like us?

"You don't *have* to come," said Matt. Ellis stopped suddenly and looked straight at Matt.

"I'd like to." Then he gave a small, quick, almost-smile. "Thanks."

They walked on to school together.

It was a fairly normal school day, really. There were the usual deadly boring bits and a very good bit, when Matt was the only one who knew the answer to a science question. Sometimes it was useful having Stuart for a brother. There was trouble at lunch time, though. Matt and Jem were eating in the canteen with a few others and Ellis was there, too, just sitting quietly, with the faraway look on his face. Joey came barging in and shouted across the room.

"Hey, it's the New Kid! Like your nice new house, do you? My dad still hasn't got a job. We might starve to death because of you!" He grinned around and a few of his mates sniggered a bit. Ellis sat staring at the table. He looked very alone. Matt felt sorry for him but he didn't want to attract Joey's attention.

Why does this keep happening? Why can't Joey and his dopey mates go and annoy someone else? All I want is a quiet life.

Joey grabbed some of Ellis' crisps and stuffed them in his mouth. "See you later, New Kid!" Then he went off to the other end of the canteen and started talking back to the dinner ladies.

"Don't take any notice of Joey," said Jem. "We call him The Mouth because he's mostly just talk. And his dad didn't lose his job because of the new houses. Mum heard; he got sacked for stealing tools." Ellis looked as though he hadn't heard her.

After school they went back to Ellis' house so he could change out of his school uniform and collect his bike. He had his own key and let himself in at the back door. They had to walk along a plank over the mud to reach it.

"C'min," he said over his shoulder and they followed him into the kitchen. Everything was shiny and new and there was a strong smell of paint. Matt and Jem waited there while Ellis went upstairs to change. It was very quiet. Only the hum of the fridge and the gentle pulse of the electric clock on the wall disturbed the silence.

"Want something to eat?" They both jumped as Ellis reappeared suddenly.

"Oh... er... OK," said Matt. Jem nodded. Ellis rummaged in a huge freezer and started ripping open packets. He shoved pizzas in the microwave and then flicked on the TV, zapping through the channels. The room was full of noise now. Then he opened a fridge the size of a wardrobe.

"Drink?" Matt and Jem stared at the huge selection of cans that filled the door.

"Will your mum mind?" asked Jem.

"No. Won't be home till later." So they filled up on pizza and fizz while the TV chattered in the background.

"So, what do you think of school, so far?" asked Jem.

"S'alright."

"Do you miss your old school?"

"No."

"I suppose you miss your friends, though?"

"Not really. Wasn't there long."

"You moved before, then?" Matt joined the questions now.

"Yeah," Ellis sighed. "Dad's jobs. This is the last time, though. Dad says. Definitely."

"That's good... isn't it?" Jem said, doubtfully.

"Was 'definitely' *last* time," Ellis muttered, staring at the TV. "Dad said we'd got to move. Mum was really mad. Hard for her to get to work now. Has to leave really early. Gets back after Dad sometimes."

"So, can you do what you want when you get home from school... if you're, like, on your own?" Matt was starting to imagine all the things he could do if his mum worked late every night.

"S'pose so."

"What do you have for tea?" Jem was very practical and knew it was important to eat properly.

"Stuff in there," he waved vaguely at the freezer.

"Wow! Pizza every night?" Matt thought this sounded great.

"If I want to," Ellis replied.

"Will your mum mind if you go out with us?" Jem wanted to be sure. Ellis shrugged.

"Not here, is she?" He sounded fed up but he didn't want them to feel sorry for him; he was just telling them how it was. Matt did feel sorry for him, though.

He's definitely lonely. If you move a lot you have to keep starting again... have to make new friends. I like it when Mum's sometimes not there when I get home, but if she was never there... I wouldn't like that. Maybe he'd like to come to Club with Jem and me.

"We need our bikes," said Matt, and he and Jem jumped up. "Wait here, won't be long."

"Thanks for the pizza," said Jem.

Ellis just nodded silently as they hurried out of the back door.

Chapter Three

"Phew!" Matt whistled. "Nice bike."

Matt was staring at Ellis' bike. It was fantastic and it looked brand new. Matt's bike had been Stuart's, and Harry's before that, and it was muddy and bashed. It still worked OK, but it was definitely not a class machine like Ellis'. Jem's was an old bike, too, and very Jem-ish; painted in yellow and purple stripes.

"Birthday present," said Ellis carelessly as they bumped their bikes over the plank and down to the road.

They squeezed their bikes through the narrow gate at the back of the churchyard.

"Over here," called Matt as they pedalled across the grass towards the back of the field.

On their way they passed some mums chatting while their little boys played football, two men walking across the field and an old lady, yelling at her dog to "Come back, or else!" The Acre could be quite a busy place sometimes. There were a few others from school already using the bike track when they arrived but there was room for three more. The track ran across some humps at the back of the field and then in and out among the trees on the edge of the wood. Next it went through a ditch, wound around some more trees before recrossing the ditch on a wobbly plank and turning back into the field again.

"Great, the swamp's really muddy!" said Jem, as she zoomed away, up and over a steep hump and then down through a huge muddy patch near the ditch on the other side. The boys followed. Soon they were all spattered with mud and Ellis' bike didn't look quite so new.

Jem was still in the lead and seemed to be glued to her bike, never losing her balance, even on the really bumpy bits. Suddenly, on the last hump, just outside the wood, she skidded to a stop. Matt was close behind and he stopped too late. Splat!

"Eeeyuck!" he spluttered through a faceful of mud. "Waddyado*that*for?"

"Sorry," said Jem, dropping her bike to come and help him. "I got distracted. Look."

The two men they had passed earlier were in the middle of the field. One of them was setting up a tripod and the other was walking away from him with a long pole.

"What're they doing?" said Matt, wiping mud out of his eyes. Jem shrugged.

"Surveyors," said Ellis, coming up behind them.

All three sat down at the edge of the track and watched the men.

"But what are they *doing*?" repeated Matt. He didn't want to admit that he wasn't sure what a surveyor was.

"Measuring the land," said Ellis.

"Why?"

"Going to build something."

"But they can't build *here*!" said Matt.

"They can," said Ellis. "If someone's bought the land."

"But Mr Cross, over at the farm, he owns most of the fields round here. He still lives in the farmhouse and he needs it," Matt protested.

"He sold the rickyard though, didn't he?" Jem reminded him.

"Yes, but that was only a little bit of the farm, just to help him because he had all that trouble when some of his cows were ill," said Matt. "Dad went to the meeting where Mr Cross explained."

"What's he use this field for?" asked Ellis.

"Nothing," Matt said.

"Could sell it then," Ellis suggested. "Room for *lots* of houses. More than where I live." The way he said it made the whole idea seem very ordinary and sensible; nothing to get worked up about, but Matt was horrified.

"Build houses on the Acre? But we *need* it!" he protested. Jem nodded.

"Loads of people use it. It's not just the bike track; we play football here and people come for walks in the wood and what about the short-cut?"

"Nice place," Ellis agreed, looking around him.

"I think we should ask," said Jem calmly, looking at the men. "No point getting worried till we know what's going on." She was always like this; no fuss, no panic.

Jem did the talking but the men weren't very helpful.

"Just doing a bit of measuring," one said when she asked, like he was talking to some really little kids.

"Could you tell us *why* you're measuring?" asked

Jem, very politely.

"For a client; a man we're working for," said the man.

"Well, could you tell us why he wants you to measure this land?"

"No, I couldn't, love. Not allowed, see? Very important man, our client is."

"But…"

"That's enough questions. Off you go now, kids: we've got work to do."

Jem stayed polite, though Matt was getting annoyed. She smiled and thanked the men and then the three of them walked back slowly to their bikes.

"That wasn't much help, was it?" Jem sighed.

"Huh, treated us like we shouldn't be out without our mums," grunted Matt.

"We'll just have to wait, I suppose," said Jem. "If anything happens we'll know because we come here all the time." Matt nodded.

"Hey, look, everyone's gone now; we've got the track to ourselves. Race you!"

He grabbed his bike and was away before the others had even reached theirs. This time he stayed in front and the others had to follow. After three circuits he slowed down and looked at his watch.

"Got to go now."

"Me too," said Jem. They walked slowly back to the gate. The men had gone now and the field was empty.

"Bye, Ellis," said Jem when they reached the road. Ellis gave them an almost-smile.

"Bye," he said. "Thanks." Then he turned and pedalled slowly back up the road.

"I think he wants to be friends really," Matt said. Jem agreed.

"Maybe he just needs a bit of practice."

As they headed for home, Matt remembered something. "Have you decided what you're doing for the history project?"

This term Mr Hicks, their history teacher, wanted them to find out about the history of their town. It could be a famous local person or place or an event that had happened there. They had all term to do it and they could present it any way they liked. Mr Hicks would keep checking up on how much work was going on so they had to get started pretty soon; no good leaving it all till the night before the presentation.

Jem nodded. "I want to find out about St Ann's church," she said, nodding towards the little old church just behind them.

There were other, bigger churches in the town, including the one that Matt's family went to. St Ann's church had been built long ago when the town hadn't spread so far and there were just a few farms and cottages nearby. It was very small and only had services once a month. Sometimes there were weddings, because it looked pretty in photographs, but mostly it was closed-up and rather sad. Not like the church that Matt went to, which was open all week, with things happening every day.

"It's a very old church and I think it looks really interesting," Jem explained. "What're you doing?"

Matt shrugged. "Dunno. I *was* going to do the Romans. When he was at our school Harry did a thing about when the Romans were here. I thought

22

I'd use that, but Mum won't let me. She says I've got to do my own work."

"We're allowed to work together, though," Jem reminded him. "You could do the church with me, if you want."

"OK," Matt agreed. "Mum might be able to get us some stuff about it from the library."

"Brilliant!" said Jem. "And my mum says she'll help if we want to make models or anything." They'd reached Jem's house. "Gotta go, bye!"

Matt leaned his bike against the side of the garage and turned the hose on hard; that way he could blast most of the mud off it without having to use a brush. Trouble was, the water bounced back, bringing the mud with it. The bike got cleaned, but he ended up wetter and muddier than ever. It would work much better if you had *really* long arms...

"Now, let me guess where you've been!" Mum was making tea when Matt squelched into the kitchen.

"Aaargh! The swamp monster's gonna get me!" Harry cowered against the wall, clutching his chest.

"Stop mucking about and get the table set," said Mum, laughing. "And trainers off at the door, *please*, Matt. Had a good day?"

"Mm. Ellis nearly got done over *twice* but, apart from that, it was OK."

There was a comfortable smell of cooking that made Matt feel glad to be home.

Ellis' house was so quiet. There was nobody there. Will his mum be there now, telling him to take off his trainers? Harry's dead annoying sometimes but I'd miss him if he wasn't here.

"Mum, me and Jem are doing St Ann's church for our history project. Can you help us get information?"

"Sure," said Mum, sliding the grill tray out and turning the sausages.

"It's very old, isn't it?" Matt asked, just checking. "I mean, old enough to be history?"

"There's been a church there for zillions of years!" Harry said, frizbee-ing place mats at the table. "I found out when I did *my* World Famous History Project on the Romans. I know loads about it and I'd be glad to help, but," he whizzed the last mat at the table, "it'll cost you, little bruv!"

"Harry, for goodness sake!" Mum protested. "I seem to remember helping *you* for free! Anyway, I've already said that Matt can't use your project; it wouldn't be fair on the others. I think the church would be a really good subject and, yes, it *is* very old. Harry's right, the building has changed over the years but people have been worshipping God on that site since Roman times. Go and wash your hands and then we can eat."

Chapter Four

After school the next day, Matt and Jem decided to go back to Jem's house to start planning their project. They waited for Ellis but couldn't find him so they left school without him. Just outside the school gates, Joey and a few others dashed past them, pushing and bouncing off other people as they went. They were kicking something along the ground in front of them.

"Ellis' bag!" said Jem. "Come on!" and she dashed after Joey and the others.

Matt didn't really want to follow her.

Oh, great! Ellis is in trouble with The Mouth again. Why can't he just stay out of their way? It's nothing to do with me... Yeah, but he's new here; he hasn't got any friends, except Jem and me. I suppose we've got to help him.

Matt saw Jem catch up with Joey. She was pulling his arm.

"What're you doing with Ellis' bag?" she yelled. "Why have you got his bag? Where is he?"

"Hoo, questions, questions!" panted Joey, laughing. "Why do you need to know?"

"Ellis is a friend, that's all," said Jem. Matt stopped nearby, but not too close. He wasn't feeling at all brave. Joey looked at Jem and laughed again.

"Friend of yours, is he? Another nutter, like you?" A crowd was beginning to gather. Matt made sure there were a few people between him and Joey.

"Yeah, her mum's that hippie woman; wears all those weird clothes," Dawn sneered at Jem. Several people laughed and Matt found he did, too; not a happy laugh, more just laughing because he didn't want to look different.

"OK, hippie kid," said Joey, kicking Ellis' school bag at Jem. "Tell your friend that he isn't welcome here and he better watch out... an' anyone who hangs round with him better watch out, an' all!" Then he and the gang all ran off, laughing.

The crowd wandered off as Matt joined Jem and picked up the bag. It was torn and dirty and something inside rattled when he shook it.

"Busted his pencil tin," he muttered, looking inside.

"Better try and find him," said Jem, looking among the crowds streaming through the school gates. "He must be still in school somewhere."

They trudged back inside but Ellis wasn't in their form room or in the corridor by the lockers.

"I'll look in here," said Matt, as they passed the boy's toilets. There he was, trying to dry his hair under the hand dryer. His face was pale and there was a bruise on his forehead.

"You OK?" asked Matt, though he could see he definitely wasn't. Ellis shrugged.

"Walk home with you, yeah?" Matt suggested. Ellis sighed and nodded.

"What happened?" gasped Jem when she saw Ellis.

"Shoved my head in the sink," Ellis muttered.

"Who did?" asked Matt, though he could guess already.

"Just... people," Ellis sounded tired.

"Joey, I suppose?" said Jem. Ellis didn't reply.

"We should tell someone," said Matt.

"NO!" Ellis shouted.

"But he's a bully—"

"Just leave it, all right?" said Ellis. "It doesn't *matter*. Forget it." And he turned and walked off.

Matt looked at Jem and she shrugged, then they ran to catch him up.

"I'm going round to Jem's house; we're planning our history project," said Matt. "Want to come?" Then he remembered. "Is that OK, Jem?"

"Yes, Mum won't mind. Have you chosen your project yet?"

"No," Ellis grunted. "Don't know anything about this place. Probably won't be here long enough to find out, either."

"You're not moving again *already* are you?" Matt asked.

"Don't know... don't care."

"But, would you like to... er... come with us to... you know... ?" Matt wasn't sure what to say. Ellis was very hard to talk to sometimes.

They had almost reached the gate into the churchyard when they heard someone yell.

"There he is! It's the New Kid. Get him!" Joey and his gang had almost reached the corner but now they turned and were stampeding back towards them.

"Quick, through here!" said Matt and they plunged through the gate and dashed around the

27

side of the church.

"Some of them're coming the other way!" panted Jem. "Must've got through the fence!"

Now they were trapped, with people on the path in front and behind.

"This way!" Matt left the path and ran round the church and across the graveyard towards a big tree that grew against the back wall. The others followed. They could hear Joey's voice, shouting instructions.

"Round the back... go *that* way!"

"In here!" gasped Matt as he flung himself at the tree and slid through a narrow gap in the trunk. The tree was huge, with branches that spread wide rather than high. Its trunk was massive and completely hollow, like a small cave. Jem and Ellis stumbled in after Matt and they squeezed themselves back against the curves of the tree's insides and waited.

"Must've gone this way."

"No one here now."

There were stomping, swishing sounds as several pairs of feet ran through the long grass nearby but no one stopped. After a while they heard the voices far away and they knew they were safe.

"Phew!" sighed Jem. "Lucky you remembered this."

"Mm," Matt felt his heart still pounding. "Haven't been here for ages, have we?"

"You OK, Ellis?" asked Jem. Ellis looked pale and scared but he managed to nod.

They climbed out of the tree and started to walk home slowly. There was no sign of Joey and the others. Ellis decided he'd come to Jem's house and as they walked they shared a squashed packet of crisps that Jem had found in her bag.

"How'd you know about the tree?" asked Ellis. He was looking better now.

"It's not really a secret or anything," said Matt. "My mum says it was hollow when she was little; it's just that not a lot of people know."

"It's very old," said Jem. "Only old trees can grow that big and be hollow and *still* be alive!"

"Could do the tree," Ellis said quietly. "The project," he explained.

"Prob'ly." Matt wasn't too sure.

"Sir said we could do anything old," Jem said firmly.

"Good; that's sorted," said Ellis.

"Clever idea!" said Jem. "Bet no one else'll think of that."

"Could we put a bit about it in *our* project about the church?" asked Matt. Ellis didn't think that would be a problem.

"We can help each other," he said. "I owe you, after today."

Yes, you do! Jem and me always seem to be rescuing you and now Joey knows we're your friends we've got to watch it, too! I didn't like what Dawn said about Jem's mum, either. She isn't weird; she's just different.

At Jem's house they had drinks and biscuits and watched TV. Sitting on the saggy sofa, surrounded by big, colourful cushions, Matt enjoyed the feeling of sitting inside a rainbow. There was coloured cellophane stuck to one of the windowpanes and the sun shone through, making bright patches on the carpet. There was a new picture on one wall, too, all bits of coloured card and glued-on string.

"That's nice," said Matt, pointing at it.

"It's an experiment," said Jem. "Mum's trying it out for college." Jem herself was busy, half-watching TV and gluing sequins onto a pair of trainers at the same time. She was always like that; making things, full of ideas, fingers busy.

Jem's mum came in. She looked just like Jem, only bigger, and she was wearing a long black velvet skirt and a shiny red top. She wore different clothes from Matt's mum but she said the same sort of things.

"I thought you were here to have a planning meeting!" she reminded them. "Turn that TV off and get to work!"

Matt and Jem decided to present their project as a display, with pictures and photos and written bits stuck onto card, and probably a model as well. Ellis wanted to type his on his computer and make it into a book. He said his dad had a digital camera, too, and that they could probably borrow it. The idea of the project seemed a lot more interesting than it had earlier.

"Well, we've got started at last," said Jem. "But we need to start collecting information."

"We need to go to the library next," said Matt.

"When's your mum going to be working in there?" asked Jem.

"Saturday morning. She said she'd help us."

They agreed to meet on Saturday and then it was time for Matt and Ellis to go home.

Halfway through tea Matt was starting to get that

'invisible' feeling again. Stuart was telling Dad how good it would be if they had solar powered heating and Harry was still going on and on about the guitar he wanted to buy, and trying to persuade Mum to lend him some money. No one was talking to Matt. Only Matt heard the soft thud as the local paper landed on the doormat. He slid off his chair and went to the front door to fetch it. He read the front page as he walked back into the kitchen. Thick, black headlines yelled at him.

**'Shelley's Farm to sell for housing?
Local farmer in planning row!'**

"Oh no!"
Everyone stopped talking and looked at Matt.
"What is it?" asked Dad as Matt passed him the paper. "Phew!" Dad whistled, his eyes flicking down the smaller print. "Looks like Mr Cross may be selling the whole farm this time."

Chapter Five

Everyone was talking at once, again; questions flying at Dad from all directions. He finished reading the front page of the paper and passed it to Mum, while Stuart and Harry tried to read over her shoulder.

"Mr Cross can't sell Shelley's Acre, can he?" Matt asked Dad, quietly. Dad shrugged.

"I'm not sure. If he owns the land I guess he can sell any of it that he wants to; but I think there are rules about what the land can be used for."

"*More* new houses!" said Stuart. "This area is going to be covered in them; not a blade of grass left anywhere!"

"But people have to live somewhere," Mum reminded him.

"OK, but the houses don't fit in," he protested. "The builders ought to use designs that are *sympathetic* and bricks that match the older buildings in the town."

"I agree," said Dad. "New buildings should fit in with their surroundings and those new houses in the rickyard look like they've been built out of Lego!"

Who cares what the houses look like; what about the Acre? If it gets sold there's nowhere else near here where we can ride our bikes and play football.

We need it!

"I don't want the Acre to have houses on it!" said Matt.

"There'll be a public meeting for local residents, I expect," said Dad. "Something like this will have to be discussed properly. Everyone living nearby will be notified; we'll have our chance to tell the council what we think. Don't worry; whatever happens will take a long time. These things usually do."

Dad hurried off to answer the phone and Stuart and Harry disappeared to their rooms. Matt helped Mum clear the table and start the washing up.

"You're very quiet tonight," said Mum. "Is it just the news about the farm or is there something else?"

Matt was quiet for a bit longer and then he decided to tell Mum.

"It's Ellis. I'm trying to be friendly, but it's *really* difficult."

"I thought you and he were getting on well," said Mum, as she stacked dirty dishes.

"We are, but... he's always in trouble."

"Oh dear, what does he do?"

"Nothing really. It's these other kids; you know, Joey Murdoch and his mates? Well, they don't like him and they keep doing things to him."

"Poor Ellis. That's a bit tough, isn't it? Especially with him being so new to the school. Sounds like he needs some good friends to stand up for him."

Matt sighed and then started to collect up the place mats.

"Me and Jem have tried to be friendly, but if Joey knows we're friends with Ellis he'll start on us, too!

They've started calling Jem a hippie, just because she and her mum dress a bit different. And... I don't like it. I don't think I can go on helping Ellis if Joey's going to have a go at me, too."

Mum stopped what she was doing.

"It's awful when people tease you, isn't it? What would you like to do?"

Matt thought.

"Pretend I don't know Ellis... or... beat up Joey to stop him being a bully!"

"And that would solve the problem, would it?" asked Mum, smiling a bit.

"Might solve *my* problem," said Matt.

"But what about Ellis getting a hard time from Joey... and what about Joey? I wonder why he's being such a bully?" said Mum. Matt shrugged; he hadn't thought of that. Mum squirted washing-up liquid into the sink. "We can't live in safe little boxes, away from people we don't like. God wants his people to live in the world and help to make it a better place."

"But I don't want Joey calling me stupid names and doing horrible things to me, too!" Matt said loudly.

"Of course you don't," said Mum, scrubbing hard at a plate. "I wonder what Jesus would do?"

"He was always good," Matt grunted. "It was easy for *him* to be brave because he had God to help him!"

"Well, so have you. How about asking God to help you, too?"

S'pose I could. I do want to stay friends with Ellis but I don't know how to do it and I'm dead scared of Joey; he's much tougher than me! Jem's braver but we both need help with this. Maybe I'll see what God can do.

"Me and Jem and Ellis are going to the library on Saturday morning. Can you help us find out things for our project?" Matt started drying dishes.

"I'll do what I can," Mum promised. "It's sometimes quite busy on Saturdays but I can show you where the local history section is and that'll get you started."

"Ellis wants to write about the old tree in the churchyard," said Matt, polishing a saucepan lid.

"Oh, St Ann's Yew; it's a wonderful old tree. Do you know, it's supposed to be a thousand years old. That's about halfway back to when Jesus was born."

Matt was impressed. "That's *lots* of history!"

"Yes, just imagine all the things that have happened here since that tree was planted," Mum agreed. "A thousand years ago there were probably hardly any houses here at all. The Romans had gone back to Italy and there would just be a few farms and little villages. There was a church here but it would have looked different from the way it does now. We'll see what we can find out."

Matt began to feel quite enthusiastic.

"It's good we've got you to help," he said. Mum went on dunking dishes in the sink.

"It'll be the same as it was for Stuart and Harry, you know," she reminded him. "I'm not doing too much. If I did then I'd want to put *my* name on the project, too!"

On Saturday the three of them met at the library. It wasn't very busy so Matt's mum was able to spend some time with them, finding books on local history and showing them how to look up the contents and index pages to see if there were any references to St Ann's church. They found quite a lot of useful books and decided to take out one each so that they could look at them properly at home. They also photocopied some old photos and a map and visited the local history society's website. Later, outside the library, they wondered what to do next.

"Mum said I could stay in town till twelve o'clock," said Jem.

"I can stay till about then, too," said Matt. "How about you, Ellis?"

Ellis shrugged. "Dad's at work; Mum's shopping. Doesn't matter when I go home."

They wandered through the shopping centre, looking in the computer games shops and waving at Harry who was wiping tables in Planet Pizza.

"Ice cream?" asked Ellis as they passed Super-Duper Scoop. Matt and Jem had spent all their money on the photocopying.

"I'll pay."

"Are you sure?" asked Jem. "It's a bit expensive."

Ellis had loads of money and he seemed really keen to spend it, so they all chose and he paid.

"Where to now?" asked Matt, carefully carrying his triple scoop (banana, chocolate chip and raspberry ripple with marshmallow topping and sprinkles) away from the counter.

"Oh, look!" said Jem. "The mime artist is back!"

They wandered through the crowd and watched

as a man in a silver suit and silver face paint pretended to be a robot; moving in jerks when you weren't expecting it.

"Hey, look who it is!" said a loud voice near Matt's ear. It was Joey and Dawn with some others. They crowded round, pushing and shoving.

"Give us a lick, then!"

"Eeeyuk, don't touch anything those weirdos are eating!"

Joey nudged Ellis so hard that his ice cream fell off its cone and splattered on the ground.

"Ooops, oh *dear*, you seem to have dropped your ice cream, New Kid!"

Matt felt scared but he just stood and watched, wishing he could be invisible.

"Push off, Joey, *please*," Jem said firmly, though she kept smiling.

"Nah, don't think I will, hippie kid. We can stay here if we want to. If you don't want to breathe the same air as us *you* can go, can't you!" He shoved Ellis again. "Eh, New Kid? You can go, can't you? Eh? Eh?"

"Look, just leave him alone!" Jem shouted and she actually shoved Joey back.

Matt had never seen Jem get annoyed and he felt even more scared.

People were starting to look at them now and the man in silver had lost his audience.

"Aaargh, don't touch me, you freak!" yelled Joey.

"Eeeyuk, you'll catch something off her!" Dawn shrieked.

Matt had had enough. Without realising, he had been slowly edging backwards into the crowd.

Now he turned and started to walk away. He walked very fast and only looked back once. He could see Ellis and Jem and Joey's gang, surrounded by a crowd of people. Two security guards were hurrying towards them. Matt dropped the rest of his ice cream in a litter bin and ran.

Chapter Six

You stupid, rotten chicken! You ran away! You left them with Joey because you were scared! What kind of a friend are you?

Matt felt awful. He kept remembering Jem and Ellis, all alone in that crowd of people. He should have stayed to help. He sat on his bed, listening to the thump-thump coming from Stuart's stereo in the next room, and wondered if Jem would ever speak to him again. Friends were supposed to look after each other, not run away when there was trouble. What could he do now? Try asking God, Mum had said. But would God want to help him after what he'd just done? Matt was desperate.

Um, God? I forgot to ask you to help me before. I suppose it's too late now and I've spoiled everything but I'm really sorry... Could you still help me? I need to know what to do next because I really want to be a good friend. Thanks.

"Boys! Lunch!" Dad shouted up the stairs. Matt went down; he still didn't feel very happy but maybe food would help. Mum wasn't back from the library yet and Harry was at work till tea-time so Dad had done 'Bloke's Lunch'. All the leftovers from the fridge got tipped into the frying pan and stirred up together. With a fried egg plopped on top it was one of Matt's favourite meals.

"How's the project going?" asked Dad as they ate.

"OK. We got lots of information this morning."

"What're you doing this afternoon?"

"Supposed to be taking photos of St Ann's church. Ellis has got a digital camera."

Will he and Jem want me to go with them after what happened this morning? What if they got into trouble? What if the security guards arrested them? Will they have to go to court or something?

Stuart looked up from the book he was reading while he ate.

"Your project could be really important, you know."

"Uh?" Matt was wondering what he would do if Jem and Ellis were put in prison.

"Your project. If Shelley's Farm does get sold, your photos may be the last to show what the church looked like when it was surrounded by fields instead of houses."

"Mm, that's true," Dad agreed. "You could be making a very valuable contribution to the local history records."

"Even more important if they knock the old church down, too," Stuart added.

"Oh, no danger of that," Dad said. "It's so old it's bound to be protected."

"Huh, but they knocked down some of the buildings in the rickyard to build those new Lego houses," Stuart reminded him.

"Well, maybe they weren't old or special enough; they kept the barn and the stables, didn't they?" said Dad.

The conversation was carrying on without Matt but he didn't notice; he was thinking about

Shelley's Acre now.

People talk as if it's definitely going to happen and there's nothing we can do to stop it. I wonder if the Acre is 'protected'. If some old buildings are, maybe special bits of ground are, too.

"How could we stop someone building houses on the Acre?" he asked suddenly, interrupting a discussion Dad and Stuart had started about motorbikes.

"Sit down in front of their bulldozer?" Stuart suggested, turning back to his book.

"Go to the public meeting and say what we think, or contact our local councillor," said Dad.

"But, what can *kids* do?" Matt persisted.

"A petition," said Stuart, not even looking up from his book.

"Yes!" agreed Dad. "Get everyone who uses the Acre to sign a petition saying that they don't want any building there because it's such an important place... useful to the local community, something like that. You could do that, couldn't you, Matt?" Matt nodded.

"Yes, there are loads of people who would sign it. Maybe that would help."

Well that's one problem sorted out but what about the other one? What am I going to do about Jem and Ellis? Still want to be friends with them? Yes. Going to say you're sorry and make up? Yes. Even if they give you a seriously bad time because you deserve it? Er... yes. Is it worth it? Yes! OK, go on then!

Matt arrived at St Ann's first. The churchyard gate squeaked as he pushed it open and his feet scrunched on the gravel path. The sunlight made the walls of the church glow warmly. There was no one else about, so it was very quiet. Some sparrows were cheeping on the gutter and two butterflies zigzagged in and out of the porch. Matt sat on the step, enjoying the quiet, and watched an ant scuttling between his feet. The gate squeaked again and there were Jem and Ellis, walking towards him.

"Hi." Matt knew he had to speak at once or he'd chicken out.

"What happened to you?" Jem looked worried.

"I... I went home."

Jem smiled. "Oh, good. We thought Joey's mates had got you. It was so crowded and I couldn't see you and then the security guards came and the others took off..."

So, they didn't see me go. They don't know I was chicken... but I've got to be honest and tell them I ran away, even if they don't want to be friends when they know.

"I-was-scared-and-I-ran-off-and-left-you-sorry," said Matt, very quickly.

"Don't blame you!" Ellis said. "I would've, too. My problem, not yours."

"But I'm your mate and mates should look after each other."

"Be my friends, you'll have trouble," sighed Ellis.

"We're not going to let Joey stop us being friends with you, are we Matt?" Jem interrupted.

"No way!" Matt answered very firmly. "From now on we stick together!" He felt happy now; it was a relief to have things sorted out.

"Right, let's get on with these photos, then," said Jem, sounding very organised. So they walked

42

around the churchyard, stopping while Ellis took photos of the church from different angles. Jem wanted close-ups of the door and some of the windows and walls to show details better. Later Matt paced out the measurements of the building, so that they could make a scale model for their display and then he joined Jem and Ellis who had gone to photograph the old tree.

"Mum says it's called St Ann's Yew and it's about a thousand years old," he said, looking at its huge, thick trunk and stretching branches.

"A millennium," muttered Ellis as he fiddled with something on the camera.

"Yeah, and like Mum says, that's halfway back to when Jesus was born," Matt added.

"Wow, 'halfway back to Jesus'!" Jem laughed, patting the rough, patchy bark. "That's *old*. My brain hurts just thinking about it!"

"What'll happen to it if they start building houses all round it?" Matt was worried. "It might get damaged."

"It's inside the graveyard wall," Ellis pointed out. "Roots could get damaged, though. Might dig too near it on the other side. Tree roots spread as wide as the branches," he added, and they all looked at the branches that swept over the wall and out into the field beyond.

"It's *so* old," said Jem. "We've *got* to keep it safe! That's another reason why they mustn't build on the Acre."

"We could do a petition." Matt had remembered Stuart's suggestion.

"What's that?" asked Jem. Matt explained, and she and Ellis thought it was a good idea.

"Could print copies on my computer," Ellis offered.

Matt had the notebook for writing down the measurements of the church so they sat down under the tree and worked out what they would say on the petition. It took a while to decide but at last they were all satisfied.

Save Shelley's Acre!!!

We are people who use the Acre all the time. If you build more houses there we won't have anywhere to play football and things because we aren't allowed to go to the leisure centre because it's too far away. Also people won't be able to take their dogs to run about. Also there is a very old tree in the churchyard and it must not be damaged.

This is very important!

"That's really good," said Jem.

"Now, all we need is millions of signatures and everything'll be all right," Matt agreed. He hadn't felt so happy for days.

Chapter Seven

Ellis typed out the petition after they'd finished at St Ann's. He made it look really eye-catching, with bright colours and a fancy border and then he printed several copies so that they had space for hundreds of signatures.

Matt took a copy home to show his family and they took it to church on Sunday. Stuart had been very enthusiastic and had got all his friends to sign it, but Harry wasn't keen.

"More houses means more customers," he'd reminded them.

News of the petition began to spread. Jem's mum was very interested and she and Jem got all their friends and neighbours to sign it. But Ellis didn't want one.

"Don't know our neighbours yet," he said. "I'll help you with yours."

"Everyone in the class has signed!" said Matt on the following Monday. During their history lesson, Mr Hicks had let them explain about the petition to the whole class.

"A very good idea," he said when they'd finished. "We need to do all we can to protect our environment from unnecessary damage!" and he was the first to sign his name. Then he finished the lesson early so that the rest of the class could sign straight away, before break.

"Let's get more signatures," said Jem. She was getting quite excited.

"Sir said we can stand at the gates after school, too," Matt added. "We can get loads more then." So they spent the rest of break collecting signatures and soon it seemed as though the whole school was talking about Shelley's Acre.

At tea-time that evening Matt was bursting to tell Mum and Dad about the petition but he had to wait. Harry was there and he had a *lot* to say, Dad had two phone calls while they were eating and Mum was kept busy trying to referee every time Stuart started a new argument with Harry. Time to be invisible for a while. At last Harry and Stuart left to do important big-brotherish things, Dad came back to his half-eaten meal and Matt felt a blanket of peace and quiet settle over the table. Mum smiled across at him.

"Hello there! You look like someone with something important to tell us. I think now might be a good time."

Matt told them how they'd got on with the petition.

"We've got over a hundred signatures from school already, just on one sheet of paper. We'll have hundreds and *hundreds* if we fill all the sheets! So many people want to save the Acre, they won't be able to build on it now, will they?"

"Well, we can't be certain yet." Dad sounded cautious.

"There are so many rumours flying about the

46

town," added Mum. "No one's really sure what's going to happen yet." Matt's happy mood felt like it had a slow puncture and he drooped in his chair.

It's no use. We're only kids. What good will we be able to do?

"There's a public meeting next week and then we'll find out who's buying the land and what their plans are," Dad said.

"When they hear about your petition they may change their minds," said Mum, trying to be encouraging.

Dad nodded. "Yes, and well done for trying. We're really proud of you."

It was Club night and Baz and Steffi had organised a Crazy Olympics competition. You didn't need to be sporty or fit, so even people with three left feet had a chance of winning something. Matt's team had won the Couch Potato Relay; pushing each other up and down the hall in one of the old armchairs from the church lounge. Then Jem came second in Chubby Bunnies. She managed to keep twenty marshmallows in her cheeks without swallowing. Later Baz did a talk about how, long ago, God helped a man from the Bible called Gideon to be brave and fight a huge enemy army called the Midianites with only a few soldiers. He said that most people didn't have to fight huge armies of enemies these days but everyone had things in their lives that felt big and scary. He said that if you trusted God like Gideon did he could help you cope. That reminded Matt about Joey and about trying to be a better friend for Ellis from now on. Joey wasn't really very big; he just seemed big because he was so loud.

"I'm never, *ever* eating another marshmallow as long as I live!" said Jem as she and Matt sat on the wall outside the church hall, waiting for her mum to collect them. "I felt *awful*... but I wasn't sick!" she added proudly. She was twiddling the end of a long braid that her mum had done in her hair. It was bound tight with rainbow stripes of thread and had a pair of tiny beads at the end. Some of the girls at Club wanted their hair done too, so Steffi was going to get Jem's mum to come and show them how she did it.

"Pity they wouldn't let us do that armchair race out in the car park," said Matt. "We'd have been mega quick... speed of light... brilliant!"

"Hey, it's the hippie's kid!" someone yelled from across the street. It was Joey and two of his mates; they'd just come out of the chip shop. Jem just ignored them but Matt watched anxiously as they sauntered away, scoffing chips and chucking the papers about.

"Phew, they've gone," he muttered, as they turned the corner. Jem didn't seem bothered and sat kicking her heels against the wall.

"Joey's just a loud mouth," she said calmly. "I feel a bit sorry for him really."

"Don't you mind when they call you... things?"

"Yes!" For a moment Jem looked upset. "Specially when they say things about Mum; I think her clothes are *beautiful*!"

"Me too," Matt agreed. "Your mum's great."

Jem cheered up. "She's my mum and I *know* how nice she is. I think if you really know someone properly then maybe you wouldn't go round saying horrible things about them."

"Same as Ellis, perhaps," said Matt. "We know he's OK, but Joey and that lot just think 'Oh, there goes that new kid from the posh new houses, we don't like him because Joey's dad lost his job.'"

"Which is rubbish because Ellis' house didn't make Joey's dad lose his job."

"Yeah, so if they knew Ellis better they might stop getting at him," Matt finished. "But that's never going to happen, is it?"

"Gideon whacked the Midianites; I don't think he thought *that* would ever happen!" said Jem, jumping off the wall as her mum's car pulled up beside them.

For the rest of the week they were busy collecting signatures for the petition wherever they went. Ellis had to print more copies and they were late home some afternoons because they had a queue of people at the school gate, waiting to sign.

"I think everyone in the school has signed by now," said Matt on Friday as they walked home. It had been raining and the path was full of puddles. "Even Taffy signed it today!" Mr Welch, the caretaker, was the biggest grouch on the planet but he had stopped them in the corridor and asked if he could sign.

"And he actually *smiled* afterwards!" added Jem.

"*He* hasn't signed yet," muttered Ellis quietly, looking over his shoulder. Matt's heart bounced hard against his ribs as Joey appeared with the usual crowd around him.

Any chance he hasn't noticed us? No, here they come. Oh, please, can I be invisible right now!

Come on, you're not going to leave the others this time, are you? Anyway, this army isn't so big... er, is it?

"Well, look who it is!" said Joey, grinning round at his mates. "Hey, New Kid, that's a nice bike I saw you riding. Hope nothing happens to it; know what I mean?"

Ellis walked on, ignoring him as usual. Joey didn't like that so he swung his school bag and bashed Ellis so hard he nearly fell over. "Don't ignore me, New Kid!"

"Give it a rest, Joey," said Jem, smiling and trying to calm things down.

"You can shut up, 'an all!" Joey shouted at her.

"OK, but just stop it, all right? We're not doing anything to you." Jem was still being reasonable.

"Eyeugh, Joey, don't talk to the hippie's kid; she might put a *spell* on you!" squawked Dawn and she flicked Jem's braid and laughed right in her face. Someone else grabbed Ellis' school bag. The strap broke and it fell in a puddle. Ellis picked it up and held it to his chest. He didn't look scared, just really tired and fed up. Water dripped off his bag and down his trousers. Joey pointed at him and screamed with laughter.

"New Kid's wet himself!"

The others all joined in, laughing and pointing.

Matt couldn't stand it any longer. "Look, just push off, all of you!" he yelled. "Go and... and borrow a brain! You're just a bunch of losers!"

Joey looked a bit startled for a moment but then he recovered.

"Huh! Think you're hard, do ya? We saw you and the hippie's kid outside the church. You go to *church*! Only weirdos go to church!"

"Weirdo! Weirdo!" The gang danced around Matt, pushing him against Jem and Ellis. The three of them stood still and waited for it to stop. None of them pushed back; it was as though they'd all agreed that this was how they'd be. Joey didn't seem to know what to do next; he hesitated. "Let's go!" he said suddenly and ran off down the road. "*You're* the losers!" he yelled over his shoulder.

The rest of the gang followed and, as they turned the corner at the end of the road, they were still yelling "hippie!" and "weirdo!" and laughing loudly. When they'd gone Ellis sighed and set off down the road. Jem and Matt exchanged 'what'll we do now?' looks.

"Want to come back to my place?" Matt suggested.

"OK," said Jem. Ellis said nothing but he turned and plodded along beside them, back to Matt's house.

Well, I didn't run away this time and I hope that shows Ellis I really am his friend. Thing is, now Joey knows, too. Pity he saw me and Jem outside church the other night... Weirdo? I'm not a weirdo! I didn't think being friends with someone could cause so much trouble!

Chapter Eight

On Saturday morning Matt was cleaning out the guinea pig's hutch. This was one of his jobs. Harry was nearby, tinkering with his bike. He was wearing his Walkman and humming loudly to himself. Matt had been thinking about Shelley's Acre a lot. It worried him that Mum and Dad didn't seem very sure that the petition would definitely keep the land safe. Surely, if hundreds of people asked you not to do something, you'd have to listen to them, wouldn't you? He gathered up the old newspaper and sawdust from the bottom of the hutch and screwed it into a bundle. Harry's bike was propped against the dustbin.

"Shift your bike, Harry."

"Na-na-na-nah, na-nah-nah..." Harry didn't hear.

"Ha-REE!" Matt prodded him.

"Wha—?" Harry looked round. "Careful! Don't go dropping sawdust, I've just oiled the chain."

"Well, shift it then!"

Harry dragged his bike away and Matt shoved the newspaper into the bin, slamming the lid with a thud. Harry pulled off his headphones and stared at Matt.

"What's got into you, little bruv? Your 'Save our Precious Bit of Grass' campaign not going very well, is it?"

"Shut up, pizza face," Matt muttered. He knew Harry was only joking but the danger to Shelley's Acre wasn't something to joke about.

Harry leant his bike against the fence; he could see that Matt was upset. "It's the public meeting on Tuesday night; then we'll know what's really going to happen," he said kindly.

Matt needed to talk to someone; even Harry might do. "But what if the petition doesn't do any good?"

Harry thought for a moment. "Hmm. I thought Boff-Brain's petition idea might not work. What you need to do, if they start building on the Acre, is take Direct Action!"

"What does *that* mean?"

Harry folded his arms, looking pleased. He enjoyed sounding brainy when Stuart wasn't around to interrupt him.

"What you do is find ways of stopping them from doing the actual work. You know, camp in the woods, build a tree house, dig a tunnel, like that bloke on TV."

"What good would that do?" Matt thought Harry's ideas sounded crazy.

"Well, they can't cut trees down if people are living in them," Harry explained. "And the tunnel bloke stayed underground for ages so they couldn't start digging. He actually stopped a whole road from being built!"

Tree houses? Tunnels? You'd need loads of stuff to build things like that. Where would we get what we needed and would it be any good if we did?

"Hey, wake up; Sid's waiting for a new carpet!"

53

Harry pointed at the guinea pig who was standing on the bare floor of his hutch, looking a bit fed up. "Better wait till after the meeting before you start doing anything too drastic, eh?" he added.

Quickly Matt spread newspaper and sawdust on Sid's floor, topped-up his food dish and checked the water bottle. Then he dashed off to meet Jem and Ellis to do some more work on their projects. They were going well, but there was still a lot to do, and the library books were due back soon. They were meeting at Ellis' house because he had the best computer and could print the photos they'd taken at the church.

The rolls of turf had been laid in Ellis' front garden now, making it look as smooth as a snooker table. There was a front path, too, but the drive was only half-finished. Inside, the house still smelled of new paint. Jem was sitting in the kitchen eating biscuits and the TV was jabbering in the corner. There was no sign of Ellis' parents.

"Dad's at work; Mum's shopping. Want a drink?" Ellis said, opening the fridge.

Later, he led them to a room with a big desk, filing cabinets and shelves of books.

"Wow, brilliant!" gasped Matt, staring at the brand new computer.

"Will your dad mind?" asked Jem.

"No," Ellis replied as he switched it on and fetched the camera. "Hardly uses it; it's mine really."

The computer chuntered gently as Ellis tapped at the keyboard.

"What do you think?" he asked as he flicked through the photos of St Ann's church and the old yew tree.

"Hey, some of these are really good!" said Matt.

"Let's have that one and that one because they show the church from opposite directions." Jem was very organised and seemed to know what they needed. Matt was too busy imagining what it would be like to have a computer like this one all to himself.

"This library book says that there might have been a Roman villa with a farm somewhere near here in about AD 200," said Jem later, when they'd printed out the pictures they'd chosen. "And they think that there was probably some kind of church where St Ann's is then, too."

"But the Romans didn't believe in our God," said Matt. "They had lots of different ones; we did it ages ago at school, remember?"

"By AD 200 lots of people had heard about Jesus and believed in God," Jem explained. "The book says that Christianity spread and spread around the world and some of the Romans who came to Britain would have been Christians."

"But St Ann's church doesn't look like a Roman building," Ellis pointed at the photos. "Roman buildings were a different shape."

"Oh, the church that's there now isn't Roman," Jem explained. "There have probably been lots of buildings there, one after the other. The one that's there now has bits that were built in AD 1000, but most of the building isn't as old as that."

"Eight *hundred* years later!" gasped Matt, doing a quick sum in his head. "That's still really old, though!"

"So, the church was built about the same time as the tree was planted," Ellis said. "I checked, the tree *is* about a thousand years old," he added.

"Do you think, one day, someone just said, 'I know, let's plant a yew tree next to our new church'?" said Jem.

"There's a bit about the tree in here," Ellis explained, holding up a book on local history. "Probably started as part of a hedge, to keep farm animals out of the churchyard."

"And it grew bigger than the rest of the hedge?" Matt suggested.

"Maybe," Ellis agreed. "It was useful. Made longbows out of its branches. Yew's strong and straight."

"Phew, you know a lot," said Matt. He was really impressed.

"There was an old photo in my book of people standing beside the tree when Queen Victoria visited the town," said Jem. "It looked old then, too."

"Pity you couldn't take photos long ago," Matt said. "Then we could've seen how big the tree was at different times and what the different church buildings looked like."

"Perhaps we could sort of imagine it and draw pictures with people wearing the right clothes standing in the churchyard?" Jem suggested.

"Can't draw," said Ellis.

"I'll do them," offered Jem. "You've done photos for us, so that'd make it fair."

Matt was feeling more and more uncomfortable. Jem and Ellis seemed to be doing all the work!

"Shall I start typing out the information neatly?"

he said.

Our old computer should just about be able to manage that! Wow, fancy having your own computer and not having to wait till Professor Boff-Brain finishes using it for his oh-so important homework.

Jem, being the organised one, made a list of all the jobs that needed doing and then they shared them out. It looked as though the two projects were starting to join together.

"I don't think Sir would mind if we share some of the information," said Matt.

Ellis agreed. "Our projects belong together. Church and tree've been together for a thousand years."

"I wonder how much longer they'll last," said Matt gloomily. "It's the meeting about the Acre on Tuesday night; Mum and Dad are going."

"My Mum is, too," Jem said. Ellis said nothing.

Matt told them what Harry had said about taking Direct Action.

"Hey, I like the idea of living in a tree house!" Jem was enthusiastic. "We could get bits of wood and build a platform and make a rope ladder—"

"And fall down and break our necks! No thanks!" Matt wasn't keen at all. "I wouldn't mind trying to dig a tunnel, though," he admitted.

"Why don't we go over to the Acre after lunch and find a good place for a tunnel, then," Jem suggested.

"What, *today*?" Matt couldn't keep up with Jem.

"Why not? Then we'll be all ready to start digging next week, if we need to! Coming, Ellis?"

Ellis seemed to be away in a daydream but he blinked and nodded when he heard his name.

"OK. Might as well," he said.

Chapter Nine

Matt and Ellis met at the Acre after lunch, with their bikes.

"Let's wait for Jem at the bike track," Matt suggested. "Race you!" The sun had shone brightly for several days so there wasn't much mud in the swamp and the track was full of dried tyre ruts which meant you bounced and jolted instead of squishing and splashing. Twice round the track and Matt was ready to stop.

"This is no good!" He and Ellis stopped and there was Jem puffing across the grass towards them.

"Sorry I'm late," she gasped. "I was helping Mum pack the stuff she's taking to a craft fair tomorrow. Oh, no mud, pity."

Ellis had been very quiet up till now. "So, the tunnel. Where's it going... if we need it?"

They stood on the highest point of the bike track, with their backs to the Acre and the distant road and looked down into the wood that began beyond the ditch.

"It'd be easier to dig down by the ditch, near the swamp; the soil's softer," Matt suggested.

"Too wet," said Ellis. "Rain a lot and it'd flood."

"Also, it's too near the wood," Jem added. "They may only want to build out here on the grassy bit.

A tunnel wouldn't do any good so far back."

"Well, how about down there, behind the track?" said Matt. "It's a bit higher than the ditch, it's away from the wood and there's lots of bushes to hide it. You could dig into the side of this hump, here." He pointed down below their feet.

"Might work," Ellis was cautious.

They left their bikes and scrambled down the side of the hump. In some places the grass was long and there were some quite big bushes.

"Might be OK," said Ellis. He somehow seemed to be in charge now. They had stopped behind the lowest hump, where the track started. "It's higher than the ditch. No one'd see us digging. Bushes'd cover us."

"Good thinking!" Jem agreed.

"But can we dig here, or is the earth too hard?" Matt wanted to know. They found sticks and sharp bits of stone and started to scrape behind the bushes.

"We need proper spades and things," said Jem, throwing down her stick.

"Tools in our garage," Ellis offered. "My house is nearest. Won't take long to get some."

Jem stayed to look after the bikes while the boys ran to Ellis' house. They came back with a spade, a trowel and a small fork.

"This is better!" said Matt, a bit later. He had dug quite a deep hole into the side of the hump.

"The earth isn't too hard, is it?" Jem said, as she scraped away the earth that Matt had dug.

"Not too far down," Ellis was still in charge. "Change direction now. Dig *into* the hump." He turned to Jem. "Spread the earth out – so people don't notice we're digging."

After a while Ellis took a turn with the spade and the other two did the scraping and spreading.

"Hey, but we aren't starting a real tunnel yet, are we?" Matt reminded them. Ellis stopped digging and looked at the hole.

"Not bad," he commented. "Won't take long to make it better... if we need to."

"What's this?" Matt was scraping the last bit of loose earth out of the hole and his trowel had hit something hard.

"Treasure?" laughed Jem.

"Nope... a hub cap, or maybe a lid, like for a dustbin." Matt pulled it out and banged the earth off it.

"Use it to cover the hole," Ellis suggested. They leaned the lid against the hole and, because of the bushes in front, you couldn't tell there was a hole there at all.

"Maybe we won't need to dig a tunnel," said Matt, hopefully.

"So many people have signed the petition, surely that'll make a difference," Jem agreed.

"Wait till Tuesday; then we'll know," Ellis reminded them as he gathered up the tools and walked back to his bike.

Four days later, everyone knew.

"Twenty houses on the Acre!" Matt was horrified.

"Well, that's what they want to build," said Dad at breakfast time on Wednesday morning. The public meeting had gone on very late and Matt had been asleep by the time Mum and Dad got home.

"But how can Mr Cross do that?" asked Matt.

"He won't be," Dad replied. "He's sold the land to the company that built Ellis' house in Rickyard Close. Shelley's Acre belongs to Smart Homes now."

"Mrs Brewer, our local councillor, did her best," said Mum. "She got someone from English Nature to come and look at the Acre."

"What for?" asked Harry.

"Well, if we could say that there was something rare living there, like a special insect or even an unusual plant, that would mean the land had to be protected."

"Like the Giant Three-eyed-Sheep-Eating Toad?"

"Something like that, yes. Unfortunately, they couldn't find anything unusual at all, so that idea didn't work."

"She also got an historian to visit," added Dad.

"But that wasn't any good, either," said Mum. "Shelley's Farm is old but the buildings aren't old enough to be really special."

"But what about the petition?" Matt said when there was finally a gap in the conversation.

"That was all taken into account," Dad sighed. "But, unfortunately the need for housing is more important than keeping that land as an open space."

Matt sat staring into his cornflakes in a cloud of gloom.

"Shame about the Acre," said Harry, shovelling cereal into his mouth. "But it'll boost Planet Pizza's sales."

"Shut up!" Matt shouted.

"Sorry," Harry muttered. He could see that Matt

was really upset.

"It's *such* a pity to build in that lovely place," Mum sighed. "I know we need more houses, but surely there's somewhere else they could use? Like the old swimming pool near the station, for instance."

"Yes," Dad agreed. "A lot of people would find that a very convenient place to live; right in the middle of the town, near the shops and the station. I'm surprised some builder hasn't snapped it up long ago."

"If they built the new houses there then that would solve two problems," said Harry, getting into the discussion. "It would tidy up that messy part near the station and mean that the Acre could stay like it is. Simple! Why hasn't somebody already thought of that?"

"Huh, it's obvious!" Stuart grunted. "It's much easier and cheaper to build on a nice empty field than clear away a broken down building."

"Much better for the environment, though," said Harry, who seemed to be changing sides.

"Since when did you care about the environment? All you think about is selling junky pizzas..."

As usual, Harry and Stuart were taking over.

"Doesn't anyone really care about the Acre?" sighed Matt sadly.

"Oh, yes!" Mum said. "Lots of people spoke out against the building last night. Some of them got really angry and the chairman had to keep shouting 'Order! Order!' It was quite exciting."

"But they're still going to take the Acre away from us," Matt pointed out.

"Well, it's not absolutely definite," said Dad. "There'll be a chance for us to appeal."

I think Dad's trying to make me feel better, but it seems as though it's no good trying to stop the building. We worked so hard on the petition and so many people signed it. It's not fair!

Matt stared at his soggy cornflakes, feeling miserable.

"Cheer up, little bruv!" whispered Harry. "If they *do* start building you can do like I said – you know... !" And he winked and pretended to dig with his spoon.

"What?" asked Mum.

"Nothing, Mum," Harry grinned. "I'm just giving Matt some advice."

"Now, I wonder why that worries me?" said Mum, looking at him suspiciously. Matt sighed and stirred his cornflakes into mush.

I think Harry cares about the Acre really, and he's trying to help. Lots of people signed the petition but it seems like it's only me and Jem, and maybe Ellis, too, who are actually doing anything. If Smart Homes won't take any notice of angry grown-ups I don't think us three have a chance! Hang on though. The Midianite's army was much bigger than Gideon's but it was Gideon's lot who won the fight... Hmm, maybe we need to start tunnelling?

Chapter Ten

"An excellent start, Ellis!" Mr Hicks had been checking, like teachers do, to see if everyone had actually started their history projects yet. "This isn't the sort of thing you can leave till the day before it's due in, you know," he reminded them. He seemed to be pleased with most people, though, and he singled out Ellis in particular. "Ellis only moved here this term and he's made more effort than some of you who've lived here all your lives. It's well planned and even his notes are beautifully presented... well done!"

Matt was pleased for Ellis and gave him a thumbs-up across the classroom but there was a low growling noise from Joey's part of the room. Ellis smiled faintly but he didn't look all that happy. At break Jem joined them.

"Well done, Ellis!" she said.

"Thanks," Ellis shrugged then changed the subject. "I heard about the meeting last night. So much for the petition; what do we do now?"

"It might not happen," Jem reminded him.

"Yeah, but they built *my* house without anyone stopping them. Shelley's Acre is just like Rickyard Close, only bigger," said Ellis. He looked grim.

"It's not *your* fault, Ellis," said Jem kindly.

"Live in one of the new houses, don't I? Feel like

people are blaming me."

"Only people like Joey," Jem insisted. "Only people who don't *think*!"

"Still wish I could do something to help," Ellis sighed.

"Who typed the petition? Who helped us find a place to dig the tunnel?" Jem was determined to cheer him up.

"Smart Homes haven't taken any notice of us so far," said Matt. He had been thinking while the other two talked. "Maybe we need to *make* them."

"You mean start a real tunnel or something?" Jem asked.

"Mm, yes. Harry says it's the only way to make people listen to you," said Matt, though he wasn't sure if it was a good idea. "We might get into trouble."

"How can we?" said Jem. "We won't be damaging anything." She was getting really excited about the idea. Matt sighed.

"OK, I suppose it won't hurt to get started." He turned to Ellis. "You still in on it?"

"Sure." Ellis started to look livelier. "Want to borrow our tools again?"

They arranged to meet after school.

It was a warm evening and they had been digging on and off for ages. Straight after school the three of them had gone home to change and then met behind the bike track with a collection of spades and a big bucket. They had been careful not to attract attention and had worked under the cover of the bushes with a short break for tea.

"Ow! My arms are aching!" said Jem. The boys

had dug out a lot of earth and it was her job to shovel it into the bucket and then carry it away and tip it in the wood where no one would notice. "I've made about ninety-six million trips and that bucket is *so* heavy," she gasped. "I'm sure my arms have stretched and I look like a gorilla!"

"I'll have a turn," Matt offered.

"No, it's OK really," Jem laughed. "I just need a rest." She flopped down beside the tunnel. "Wow, it really looks like a tunnel now!"

Ellis crawled out backwards from the tunnel and dropped the trowel he'd been using. He was filthy but then so were Jem and Matt. Jem's dungarees now had dirty brown knee patches instead of red stripy ones and they all had dirty hands and smudges on their faces.

"It's nearly deep enough for one of us to get right inside," said Jem, excited.

"Need some wood to support the roof and sides otherwise it may cave in," Ellis said.

"You know a lot, don't you?" said Matt. He was impressed.

"Found a website on the Internet," Ellis explained. "Showed you how to do it properly."

"What'll we use?" asked Matt.

"Builders have left loads of bits of wood near my house. Could try that," Ellis suggested.

"Hey, time I went!" said Jem, rubbing the dirt off her watch.

They tidied up carefully and propped the dustbin lid back in the doorway before they went home.

"So, what're you going to say to your mum when she wants to know why you're covered in dirt?" asked Jem, as she and Matt walked home together.

"Um, how about 'I've been helping Ellis do some gardening'?"

"Nice one!" laughed Jem. "We *have* been helping Ellis and digging is sort of like gardening... yup, that'll do!"

The digging went on for several weeks, whenever they had any spare time. They found some planks in Ellis' garden and Jem brought bits of an old fence that didn't seem to be doing anything in her garden. Ellis sawed up the long bits and then fitted them into place along the tunnel. Matt and Jem helped, but it was mostly Ellis' ideas. The tunnel was now long enough for one person to crawl into, with a sort of cave bit at the back to turn around in. There was no more news about the building and, gradually, the tunnel didn't seem so urgent.

"It's all ready, in case we need it, though," said Matt, as they covered up the entrance and crawled back through the bushes.

What was getting really urgent was the history project.

"Sir wants to see how we're getting on, so I'm taking in the pages I've typed," said Matt as he packed his school bag one morning.

"How's it going?" asked Mum.

"OK, I think. We've found out the name of the man who built the Victorian bit of the church that's there now and how much it cost. Jem's done some brilliant drawings of what some of the earlier buildings would have looked like. We've been making this model, too, with a roof that lifts off so you can see what it might have looked like inside the building that was there about six hundred years ago."

"Long ago churches used to be very colourful inside," said Mum.

"Yes, the book said they had lots of pictures of Bible stories painted on the walls," said Matt. "Because the people hadn't got Bibles of their own."

"Most of them couldn't read anyway," Mum added as she handed him his lunch box. "I'm looking forward to seeing this project when it's finished."

"There's going to be a parents' evening with a display at the end of term," said Matt.

"How's Ellis?" Mum asked.

"OK... The Mouth... er, I mean, Joey has a go at him sometimes."

"Does Joey bother you, too?"

"A bit," Matt shrugged.

"Would it help if I phoned the school?"

"No!" said Matt quickly. "We can manage!"

Matt walked to school and met Jem and then Ellis on the way. Jem was carrying a cardboard box with the church model in it.

"It's not quite finished," she explained. "But I want Sir to see that we've been busy."

"You brought anything?" Matt asked Ellis.

"Got it here." He tapped a fat folder under his arm.

"Wow, you must have written *loads*!" Matt wondered what Mr Hicks would say about his four pages of typing.

It doesn't look much but it took me ages and it was dead dangerous! I bet no one else gets half-

killed by their brother for losing his physics homework. Stuart was on the phone... I didn't mean to delete anything...

"I've just about finished," said Ellis. "Writing's done. Photos look good, Jem's drawings, too. Ow!"

Ellis stumbled and nearly fell as Joey ran past and pushed him hard in the back.

"Out of my way, New Kid!" he shouted.

Oh no, just when we thought it was safe. Why does this keep happening? Being bashed-up by Stuart is one thing, but Joey's something else!

The rest of Joey's gang caught up with him and crowded round.

"Oooh, what've you got in the box, hippie kid?" asked Dawn.

"Just something for my history project," Jem replied calmly.

"Let's have a look!"

"No, it's fragile."

"Didn't you hear what she said?" shouted Joey. "She wants to have a look!" He tried to grab Jem's box but Matt and Ellis stood in front of her. Then there was a lot of pushing and pulling and shouting. Suddenly Joey was holding something high above his head; it was Ellis' folder.

"Well, what's *this* then, New Kid?"

"My history project. Give it back... please."

"The famous history project that Sir says is better than anyone else's? Now, this I must see!"

"Oh, *please* Joey! It's really important!" Jem was begging him. Matt leapt to grab the folder but the others were holding him back. Ellis was standing like a statue; his face was very white. People were passing and staring but no one stopped to help.

Slowly Joey opened the folder and took out the wad of papers inside, then, grinning at Ellis, he began to rip them up and throw them in the air.

"Nooooo!" screamed Jem. She was still clutching her box and tears were streaming down her face. "How can you be so mean? It's taken him weeks to write all that," she sobbed.

"Huh, as if I care!" Joey smirked, still shredding paper and flinging it about. "We don't want people like *him* round here. You can take your precious project and get lost!"

He flung the empty folder at Ellis and then ran off, with the rest of the gang following. For a few seconds nobody spoke. Jem was sniffing and gulping and Matt just stood and stared at Ellis.

"Right, that's it!" muttered Ellis quietly. He turned and ran back down the road.

"Ellis, wait!" Matt shouted but Ellis ignored him.

"Better leave him. He's probably gone home to calm down," said Jem. She'd put down her box and was trying to gather up the torn pieces of paper. It was hopeless; some of them were on the road and cars were driving over them, others were stuck, fluttering in the hedge.

"What'll we do?" Matt said shakily, still staring down the road after Ellis. "We'll miss registration if we don't hurry."

Jem stuffed the bits of paper into her school bag and picked up her box.

"All that work, ruined!" Matt was thinking of how thick the folder had looked under Ellis' arm. "We'll have to tell someone at school."

"But he might not want us to," said Jem. "He

went mad last time."

"You mean, when they beat him up in the loo?"

"Yes, he really didn't want us to tell anyone, did he?"

"S'pose so, but all that *work*!"

"He'll be able to print the writing out again, I expect," said Jem, trying to sound comforting.

"But what about your pictures?"

"I could do them again. Oh, poor Ellis!"

"That Joey is *well* out of order!" Matt fumed as they hurried through the school gate. "It's time someone sorted him out properly!"

Chapter Eleven

Ellis didn't come to school for the rest of that week and by Friday Matt was uneasy. He couldn't forget the look on Ellis' face as Joey ripped up his project.

There was something about the way he said, "That's it!" as if, well, as if that really was 'it'... the end. It was like he'd finally decided something. Maybe he's never coming back!

"I just thought he was having a few days off, you know, to get over the Joey stuff," he said to Jem, on Sunday afternoon.

"Shall we go round to his house and see how he is?" she suggested. Matt had thought about this but he was a bit nervous about meeting Ellis' parents; he didn't know what they'd be like. If Jem came too it might be easier.

Ellis answered the door but he didn't seem very pleased to see them. He kept looking over his shoulder, as if he didn't want anyone in the house to know what was going on.

"Hi, Ellis. How are you?" Jem asked in her usual friendly way.

"OK," Ellis grunted, stepping out on to the doorstep and nearly closing the door behind him.

"Have you been ill?"

"Ssh!" said Ellis, looking shifty.

"What's going on?" Matt was puzzled.

Ellis glared at him. "Stop shouting!"

"I'm not—"

"Mum. In there. She doesn't know. Been skipping school."

"What?" Matt was shocked.

"Ellis, you'll get into trouble if you skip school," Jem said anxiously.

"I *know*!"

"Are you coming back?" Matt wanted to know.

"Yeah. When I've finished."

"What?"

"Something important."

"Can't you tell us? We're your friends," Jem reminded him.

"I will... soon."

"What if someone asks us about you?" Jem always thought of things like that.

"You don't know. Nothing to tell, is there?"

"S'pose not," she said doubtfully. "You won't do anything wrong, will you?"

"No. It'll be great. Really."

"But—"

"You my mates?"

"Course!" said Matt.

"Don't tell anyone. *Anything*."

Matt and Jem looked at each other and then at Ellis. "OK."

"Promise?"

They nodded.

After that Ellis almost-smiled for the first time. "Want to come in? Play 'Wacky Wrestlers'? Dad's out. We can use the computer."

Monday morning Ellis was back at school, looking

as though nothing had happened.

"Have you finished whatever-it-is?" whispered Matt as the register was called.

Ellis nodded but said nothing. Matt was bursting with questions.

Why does he have to be so mysterious? We're his friends. We look after him and keep secrets for him but he hardly tells us anything... He's had a bad time, though, hasn't he? All this moving about and new schools and now The Mouth. Maybe he finds it hard to know if he can trust us yet. I suppose we'll just have to be patient.

For the rest of the day neither Matt nor Jem asked Ellis any questions, but on the way home, just as Ellis turned into Rickyard Close, he said, "Tell you tomorrow." Then he darted off before either of them could speak.

"Huh, Mr Mystery," grunted Matt.

"I think it's exciting," said Jem, and they walked on down the road.

Just before tea Matt was watching TV when the phone rang.

"Matt, did Ellis come home from school with you today?" asked Mum. "It's his mum on the phone. She got back from work early and he wasn't there."

"He walked home with me and Jem," said Matt. "He went down his road, same as usual." Mum talked for a bit and then hung up.

"Ellis' mum says she thinks he's been home because his school uniform's in his bedroom, though he's taken his school bag. Have you any idea where he'd be?"

Matt shrugged. "He doesn't really know anyone except me and Jem. He may have gone to the library or something."

"Yes, that's what she thought. She says he often goes off without telling her. I said we'd call her back if we find out where he is." She stopped and looked hard at Matt. "Are you sure you don't know anything?"

Mum always seems to know when things aren't quite right. I've got to say something or she'll keep on asking. But we promised Ellis! Help! Oh, I know; I'll tell her about what Joey did to Ellis' project.

Mum frowned. "Oh dear, that sounds horrible. Did you tell anyone at school, a teacher, I mean?"

"No," said Matt. "Last time something like this happened Ellis went mad when we said we should tell someone. He doesn't want any fuss."

Mum smiled. "Don't worry; you did what you thought was best."

After tea there was another phone call. Matt answered this time.

"Matt?" said a strange, husky voice.

"Yeah?"

"It's me." The voice had changed; it was Ellis.

"Where are you?" Matt whispered.

"Listen! Just answer 'yes' or 'no'!" Ellis' voice sounded urgent. "I'm OK. Need your help. Get me some things, yeah?"

"Yes," said Matt cautiously.

"Need matches and a jacket. Something waterproof. You still there?"

"Yes, but where are *you*?"

"Doesn't matter. Safer if you don't know."

"Wha—?"

"Shh! Using Dad's mobile. Meet me by the old tree. In the churchyard. Can you get there without anyone knowing?"

"Er, yes."

"Good. Hurry!"

"There in five minutes!" Matt whispered.

He found a box of matches in the kitchen and stuffed it into a carrier bag with an old jacket that was hanging in the back porch. Then he ran upstairs, sneaked into Stuart's room and borrowed the torch he'd seen in there. Next came the tricky bit; getting out of the house without anyone seeing him. Dad and Harry were out and Stuart was talking to Mum in the sitting room. Holding his breath, Matt sidled past the open door then headed for the back door, grabbing his own jacket on the way.

It was getting quite dark as he ran down the road. Clouds were gathering and there was a chilly wind blowing. Matt crossed the main road and jogged through the gate and across Shelley's Acre. He needed the torch by the time he'd reached the gate into the churchyard. He could see the silhouette of the old tree, dark against the sky.

"Ellis?" he said, quietly.

"In here," said a voice out of the gloom. "Don't need to whisper; no one else around."

Ellis appeared from inside the tree trunk.

"Got the stuff?" Matt nodded and handed him the bag.

"Good. Thanks."

"Where are you going?" asked Matt.

"I'm OK," said Ellis. "Got a good place. Needed

something in case it rains; my school jacket isn't waterproof."

Matt suddenly realised. "You're in the tunnel, aren't you?"

Ellis nodded. "Starting tomorrow."

"Your mum's worried," said Matt. "She phoned our house earlier."

Ellis glanced at his watch. "She's back early. Better get home quick!" He put Matt's bag into the tree.

"Why are you doing this?" Matt asked. He could see Ellis frowning in the torchlight.

"Just got to. Think it'll help."

"What about food and things?" Matt was still worried.

"Got plenty, just needed matches for the candles."

"But... what if you need help?"

"Got the mobile. I'll call you. Leave stuff in the tree, OK?"

Matt tried once more. "Why are you doing this? I'm your mate; can't you tell me?"

Ellis shook his head. "You *really* my mate? Then don't ask questions and don't tell *anyone*, OK? Got to do this. Important. Explain later," he muttered.

It was Club night again but Matt didn't feel like joining in the table tennis tournament. He couldn't concentrate on anything.

"I'm worried about Ellis," he said to Jem.

"Do you think he's planning on skipping school again or something?"

"Maybe." Matt had to be careful how he answered Jem's questions.

"It's all that trouble with Joey, isn't it?" said Jem.

"I think that's part of it," Matt agreed.

"I wonder what he's up to."

Matt shrugged; he felt bad not telling Jem, but he'd promised Ellis he wouldn't.

"Shouldn't we tell someone?"

"No!" Matt didn't realise he'd shouted; people were staring. "No, we promised, remember?" he muttered, quietly.

"Don't worry," Jem assured him. "I haven't forgotten."

After that, Steffi came and dragged them off to play table tennis and for a little while Matt stopped worrying about Ellis and concentrated on using the dazzling forehand smash that Harry had been teaching him.

That night it rained. Matt lay awake listening to raindrops spattering his bedroom window and cars swishing down the road.

I wonder what Ellis told his mum. I wish I could tell Jem. I hope he doesn't do anything stupid... I hope... I hope...

Chapter Twelve

Next morning, Matt was still half asleep when the phone started ringing. He heard Dad answer it. Later, as he was coming downstairs, it rang again. Stuart answered it.

"Huh, no one there," he grunted, hanging up.

"Second time this morning," said Dad. Matt was suddenly very wide awake.

He was eating his breakfast when it rang again. This time he was ready.

"I'll get it!" he said and dived out of the kitchen.

"Ellis?" he whispered, hoping the noise of the radio in the kitchen would cover his voice.

"Yep. Listen. Got a bit of trouble. Can you come?" Ellis sounded breathless.

"OK, but—"

"Need a bucket and a big bit of plastic to keep something dry."

Matt was trying to think. He stared out of the window by the front door. It was still raining.

"You still there?" Ellis' voice was urgent.

"Mm," Matt replied.

"Can you do it?"

"S'pose so, but where to? The old tree?"

"No, the tunnel. Don't tell *any*one! Gotta go!"

Matt hung up the phone and went on staring out the window.

"Yo, little bruv! Wassup?" Harry bounded downstairs and patted him on the head as he passed. Matt jumped

"Nuthin'!"

Harry stared at him, hard, and Matt hurried off to find the things Ellis needed.

Why do my family always see me when I don't want them to? Usually Harry takes more notice of his guitar than he does of me and now, here he is, asking questions and giving me funny looks. I wouldn't be surprised if Stuart suddenly remembered I exist, too, and as for Mum... I'll never get past her!

Luckily for Matt, by the time he was ready to go, he was invisible again, thanks to Harry who had tried to cook a banana and jam sandwich in the toaster. The air was full of smoke and shouting voices. Matt slipped out the front door and hurtled up the road to Shelley's Acre. If he was quick he could be back before anyone noticed he'd gone.

The ground grew more and more soggy as he ran across the grass and, when he reached the bike track, he had a shock. The ditch had overflowed and now the bike track was almost completely surrounded by water. The only way to reach the tunnel, without wellies or a boat, was by going over the top. Matt scrambled up and slithered down the bank on the other side. As he worked his way along the side of the bank he had to hold on to bushes and tufts of grass to stop himself slipping down the bank and into the water.

"Ellis!" It wouldn't matter if he shouted now; there was no one to hear him. A figure appeared in front of him from behind a bush, wearing the old jacket Matt had found, camouflage trousers and wellies. Its head was almost covered in a balaclava and it was smothered in mud. Matt skidded to a halt and stared.

"Ellis?" said Matt doubtfully.

"Got the stuff?" asked the muddy figure.

"Yes, but—" There were so many questions queuing up to be asked that Matt was almost speechless.

The figure pulled off its balaclava and became Ellis, well, from the neck up, anyway.

"Oh, it *is* you!" said Matt, very relieved. "Phew, you must've got up early!"

"Yep." Ellis gave his almost-smile; he seemed quite pleased with himself. "Come and see."

He led Matt through the bushes to where they had started the tunnel. Matt had another shock when he bent down and looked through the doorway. The tunnel leading into the cave was now almost completely lined with bits of wood and the cave bit at the back looked bigger than ever. There was a big pool of water, though, halfway along the tunnel. Ellis pointed at it.

"Got a leak. Water's getting in somewhere." As he spoke, another drip fell into the puddle. "Need the bucket to put under it. And the plastic. To sit on," he explained.

"When did you do all this?" gasped Matt.

"Last week," Ellis explained. "Got it all set up now. My camp."

"But... *why?*" Matt couldn't understand. "Just because of The Mouth?"

Ellis shook his head. "Wouldn't waste my time on *him*. Going to save the Acre!"

82

Matt stared. "You mean... like the bloke Harry was talking about? The one who lived in the tunnel and stopped the road being built?"

Ellis nodded. "Been thinking. Can't help where I live. Too late to change that. Want people to see I care about the Acre, too. Gonna stop the new houses. Can't start building if I'm living here."

He seemed very certain about this but Matt wasn't so sure. "What if they get the police and arrest you or something. You could get into big trouble!"

"Worth it if it makes people listen. Got to get me first!" He ducked into the tunnel and started to pull up a sort of drawbridge made from a big bit of wood that he had cut to fit the shape of the doorway. It fitted much better than the old dustbin lid they had used at first.

"Can lock it, too!" he said proudly, showing Matt the cable and padlock from his bike that was threaded through a hole in the door and around one of the strips of wood that framed the doorway.

"What if it takes a long time?" asked Matt. "You'll need food and things."

"That's your job!" Ellis replied. Matt had begun to suspect that it might be. He sighed and handed over the bucket and the picnic groundsheet he'd found in the garage. Ellis was very pleased.

"Need more matches. Dropped these." Ellis held up a soggy matchbox.

"So, you're going to stay here, even at night – in the dark?" asked Matt, feeling more impressed every minute.

"Got to," Ellis shrugged. Matt pulled the torch out of his pocket. He felt he needed to do something else to help Ellis.

"Use this. Have you got enough food?"

"Loads!" Ellis crawled into the cave and came back with his school bag. It was bulging with bottles and packets. "Let you know when I need more."

"So, what happens now?" Matt asked. "There's no point living here if no one knows you're here."

"Going to phone the local paper," Ellis replied, sounding very efficient. "Not quite ready yet. Need to finish the door."

Matt looked at his watch. "Gotta go!" he gasped. "I'll come back after school, OK?" He paused. "Er, can I tell Jem?"

Ellis thought for a moment then nodded slowly. "Only Jem. *No one* else, right? Talk now and it ruins everything!" He looked very stern and grown up, standing there, dressed like a commando and all covered in mud. Matt almost wanted to stay with him but the cave would only hold one and, anyway, he really didn't fancy being out there in the rain all day.

"See ya!" he called as he scrambled back along the muddy bank.

Things were a bit awkward when Matt got home.

"Your *shoes*! Where on *earth* have you been?" said Mum as he slunk in the back door.

"Been feeding Sid," Matt fibbed desperately. He'd stuffed a bunch of grass into Sid's hutch as he dashed past, so it was sort of true. Mum just said "Hmm!" and gave him a look as he picked up his lunch box and school bag. The phone rang and Harry answered it.

"Mum!" he shouted. She left the kitchen and Harry came in.

"You got a school trip today?" he asked as he carried on eating his breakfast.

Matt shook his head.

"Well, your mate Ellis went off early this morning; told his mum he was going on a school trip. She's sussed him. Rung up to see if there's a letter she should have had."

Matt just grunted and finished packing his school bag.

"Wonder where he's gone?" Harry said. "He's going to be in *deeeep* trouble; his mum sounded mega stressed!"

Matt didn't wait to hear any more. He grabbed his bag and ran.

It had stopped raining and a pale sun was shining in a grey sky. Jem was just passing Matt's front gate as he ran down the path. She was wearing a very shiny purple plastic mac.

"Are you all right?" she asked, looking at his muddy shoes and red, flustered face.

"It's Ellis," he explained, and he told her about what had happened that morning.

"Wow!" gasped Jem. "*Really*? Isn't he amazing?" Then she thought for a moment. "But what about his parents? My mum would be *so* worried. I just couldn't do something like that!"

Matt began to think, too.

Yes, Ellis is doing a very brave thing but I could do what he's doing, easy! Thing is, I don't know if I'd want to. I wouldn't be scared; I just wouldn't want Mum and Dad to worry. His parents are

different, though. Ellis says they're never there.
Maybe it's OK for him because they wouldn't
care... but Harry said his mum sounded really
upset on the phone...

"I wish we could go and see him now," said Jem
as they hurried along the footpath towards the
churchyard.

"We mustn't!" said Matt urgently, as they passed
a lady walking her dog and a man with a briefcase
hurrying in the opposite direction, towards town.
"There's too many people around."

At registration Mrs Brown made a worrying
announcement.

"As some of you may have noticed, Ellis Palmer
isn't at school today. We need to know where he is.
It's quite urgent. Perhaps those of you who know
him better can give us some information?" She
glanced round the room as people turned to look at
each other and shook their heads. Some of them
stared at Matt but he just shrugged and hoped his
face wasn't going red. He didn't dare look at Jem
but he sent her a desperate thought message.

Jem, please! We mustn't say anything. Ellis said if
we talk it'll ruin everything. I promised! We
mustn't let Ellis down; he trusts us.

Chapter Thirteen

Matt found it difficult to concentrate at school for the rest of that day. Other people were talking about Ellis at break and lunch time. It was hard to keep pretending he didn't know anything. The day seemed endless. Matt felt tense, as though there was a piece of elastic inside him that was stretched too tight.

I need to talk to Jem. If I don't get away from here soon I think I'm going to go 'ping!' and tell someone else.

At last the final bell rang and he and Jem bolted for the school gate.

"We'll have to be really careful," Matt panted, as they jogged down the road, towards the church. It was hard not to hurry when they arrived at Shelley's Acre.

"If we just walk across the grass towards the bike track, like we're just going for a stroll, no one'll be suspicious," said Jem. They tried very hard to walk slowly and not keep looking around at the other people nearby.

"I feel like everybody's watching us!" Matt muttered.

"Just keep acting normal!" Jem replied calmly. She was enjoying herself.

It had begun to drizzle again as they scrambled

up and over the humps of the track, and the slopes were even more slippery. When they reached the bushes near the tunnel entrance there was no sign of Ellis.

"Maybe he's got fed up and gone home?" said Matt, but at that moment Ellis appeared through the bushes. Jem squeaked and jumped.

"'S me," said Ellis, pulling off his balaclava again.

"Everyone's been asking about you," Matt told him.

"But we didn't say anything," Jem assured him, quickly.

"Good!" said Ellis. He showed Jem the improvements he'd made to the tunnel and they took turns crawling in and out of the cave at the back. Even though the floor of the tunnel was now covered with the groundsheet Matt had brought, Matt got dirty knees and Jem tore a hole in her tights.

"You're really great, doing this," Jem said to Ellis.

He looked pale and tired.

"Don't you think you should come home now, though?" she suggested. "It's so wet and muddy here. Aren't you getting cold?"

"Nope!" Ellis pulled his balaclava on again. "Cave's OK now. Still got lots of food. Can't stop now. Nearly there."

The drizzle was turning into steady rain.

"You'd better go," said Ellis and it sounded like an order. Matt and Jem hesitated.

"Go! I'm OK! Got the mobile. Call you if I need you. GO!"

So they went.

When Matt got home Mum wasn't back from work, so he was able to clean his shoes a bit and change out of his muddy clothes without having to answer any questions. He still felt as if he had that piece of too-tight elastic inside, though. What Ellis was doing was very exciting and brave, but something didn't feel right.

What if Ellis is wrong and his mum and dad are worried? Saving the Acre is brilliant, but is it worth it if they get upset? I wish I could talk to Mum or Dad... but I mustn't tell anyone. Ellis is my friend. I promised him I wouldn't tell, and friends should keep promises.

Not long after, Mum came home. Matt stuck to his promise and didn't say anything about Ellis and the tunnel, but it wasn't easy. All through tea Matt's brain felt like a tumble drier, with his worries churning round and round. Harry was at work and Stuart was out with friends so it was unusually quiet.

"Mrs Palmer phoned again this afternoon, before I went to work," said Mum. "Ellis still hasn't come home. They've told the police."

Matt felt the elastic inside go tighter than ever.

"That poor woman, she sounded frantic!" sighed Mum. "Are you *sure* you can't think of where he might be?"

"Nymph," Matt grunted and went on eating, though he was finding it very hard to swallow.

"What's the matter?" Dad asked later, as Mum was searching in the freezer for ice cream. Matt shrugged.

"Just got a bit of a problem," he muttered.

"Can I help?" asked Dad.

Matt took a deep breath. This was going to be tricky, but he thought he could manage to get some help without letting out the secret.

"Friends should keep promises, shouldn't they?" he asked.

Dad nodded.

"What if it looked like... keeping a promise might... cause trouble?" Matt was choosing his words very carefully. Dad thought for a while.

"Hmm. That's a hard one! Well, I think if I'd made the promise before I really understood what was going on, I might have a good reason to change my mind. It might mean I was being a *better* friend if I did that. But I'd have to be really certain I was breaking my promise for a good reason."

Matt nodded. He thought he understood what Dad was saying but he wasn't sure if he had a really good reason for breaking his promise to Ellis.

All I want to do is talk to someone to see if they think Ellis is right to hide in the tunnel and not tell his parents. I'm worried. It sounds like his parents might really care about him like Mum and Dad care about me. But if I'm wrong and they don't... I'll have broken my promise and it'll spoil Ellis' plan and it'll be all my fault!

"Does that help?" asked Dad. Matt remembered where he was and blinked.

"Er, a bit... I think."

"If it's a hard decision I always talk to God about it," Dad suggested. "If you want to be a good friend I'm sure God will help you do the right thing. He's very interested in you and your friends."

Then Matt remembered that he hadn't talked to God about anything much for a while. He knew God was there, loving him and looking after him, but he kept forgetting that he could talk to him about everything. Talking to God had really helped after he had left Ellis and Jem at the shopping mall and didn't know what to do next. After tea he went up to his room and sat on the bed.

Hello, God. It's me again. Sorry I haven't been talking to you much. Dad says you know all about everything so, please can you help me to know what to do about Ellis? He's doing a really brave thing but I think it's a bit wrong, too. He shouldn't be making his mum and dad so worried... I think they might care about him more than he thinks. I also think it might be quite dangerous, I mean, what if a bulldozer came along and started digging and Ellis was in the tunnel!

Matt jumped up. He decided to have one more try at persuading Ellis to come home. If that didn't work, he'd talk to Mum and Dad.

"Just going down to Jem's," he called as he dashed out of the house. It was raining heavily now. Jem was pleased to see him when he arrived.

"Oh good! You can help me cut out these captions and mount them for our display," she said. Matt had completely forgotten about the history project!

"I'll help you later," he said. "First we need to sort out Ellis!" Quickly he explained his plan. Jem listened quietly.

"I think you're right," she agreed. "Saving the Acre is great but not if it means his parents going crazy or him being squished by a bulldozer!" She jumped up and fetched her coat. "Just going down to Matt's!" she called to her mum who was marking homework in the kitchen.

"Two rings when you get there!" called her mum. Whenever she went to Matt's house Jem phoned home and let it ring twice, just to tell her mum she'd arrived safely.

When they got back to Matt's house, Harry and his friends were having a band practice in the garage. The noise was deafening so it was easy to slip into the hall, use the phone and sneak out again without anyone noticing.

"We've got to be quick," said Jem as they ran along the road, through the rain. "I don't think Mum would like me going out like this."

"It's an emergency!" Matt panted. "And we'll be together all the time."

It was getting quite gloomy as they squelched across the grass towards the bike track. Matt felt in his pocket for the torch and then remembered that he'd given it to Ellis. Things look very different when it's nearly dark but they found their way to the tunnel without too much trouble. The door was shut but there was a thin rim of light glowing around the edges.

"Ellis!" Matt thumped on the door. There was some scuffling and then the door slowly opened. Ellis peered out at them. He was holding Stuart's torch.

"What?" He didn't look very pleased. Matt pulled his hood further forward to try and stop the rain getting in his eyes.

"You've got to come home," he said. "It's time to come home."

"No way!"

"Ellis, listen," Jem crouched down and looked at him seriously. Her hair was in rats' tails and water was dripping off her nose. "We think what you've done is fantastic but you've got to stop now. It's cold, it's wet and your mum and dad are *really* worried!"

"They've told the police!" Matt added. Ellis frowned.

"Can't give up now!"

Matt hunched into his jacket and shivered as the rain began to soak through to his shoulders.

"Please come!" he pleaded.

"No!" Ellis backed into the tunnel and began to shut the door. Matt grabbed it and they both pulled. There was a cracking sound as part of the frame snapped and the doorway sagged.

"Watch it!" shouted Ellis. "Now look what you—" He never finished because, suddenly, he wasn't there any more.

Chapter Fourteen

There was hardly any noise really, just a sort of soft, swooshing thud as the tunnel doorway crumbled and caved in. There was a heap of earth where the doorway had been. Jem gasped and jumped to grab the torch that was rolling away down the slope towards the flood below. She shone it on the earth. Matt saw two hands sticking out of the earth, twitching and flapping like a pair of starfish dancing on a rock. Then Ellis struggled out. He was spitting mud and he was very, very angry.

"Stupid... eyugh! Gone and spoilt... yuk! All your fault... pfuygh!"

He tried to stand up but couldn't. "Leg's stuck!" he snarled. "Can't get my leg... *ow*!"

"Scrape the earth away!" Jem ignored the shouting, propped the torch so it shone on Ellis' head and then joined Matt trying to dig Ellis out.

"Some of the bank has slipped like a landslide," said Matt, squinting up through the rain at the bike track.

"Stop talking! Get me out! You stupid... ruined *everything*!"

"We need help!" said Jem. They had been digging for ages and the earth was turning to mud but they still couldn't free Ellis' leg.

They looked at Ellis. He had stopped spluttering and shouting now and was shivering.

"You stay here!" said Matt, struggling out of his jacket. "I'm going home! Keep the torch; I'll manage!" He took off his jacket and put it over Ellis.

Jem nodded, scraped the hair out of her eyes and went on digging.

Matt slithered back along the bank and ran into the darkness. He remembered how scared he'd been of Joey and his gang; how they had seemed as big and scary as that huge army Gideon had to fight. That all seemed silly now. Seeing Ellis trapped in the mud was far more frightening. The rain stung his face and he shivered as he stumbled along.

It's good we know the Acre so well; I can find my way, even in the dark… well, I think I can. What if Ellis has hurt himself badly? It was better when he was shouting at us. I don't like the way he went all quiet… perhaps I should have told someone about Ellis before… I shouldn't have waited… but I promised him! Please God, help me to get home quickly… help me to sort this out! I want to do the right thing… it's an emergency… I've got to tell people about Ellis and his plan now!

It seemed to take hours till Matt staggered through his back door. Now he had no doubts; it was obvious that Mum and Dad needed to know. There wasn't time for the whole story yet but Matt was certain that he would tell it later. As he panted out his message Matt realised what a relief it was, being able to share the secret with people who could really help. Mum and Dad were great; they didn't fuss or waste time with lots of silly questions; they listened, nodded and then Dad hurried off to get torches and spades and collect Harry who was tidying up in the garage after band practice. Mum tried to make Matt stay home to get dry.

"I can't! I've got to show Dad the way!" he protested. Mum didn't argue; she found him a dry jacket and then went to phone the Palmers and Jem's mum.

"Hey, little bruv; what've *you* been up to?" asked Harry as he burst into the kitchen.

"No questions now!" said Dad briskly. "Grab a spade and a torch and come with us!" It was amazing; Harry didn't argue; he did just what Dad asked.

"Hurry, *hurry*!" Matt gasped as he ran back up the road towards Shelley's Acre with the others.

"Jem! We're here!" Matt dashed ahead along the side of the bank. The dark wasn't a problem now; he had a torch so he could see where he was going. He thought for a moment that he was in the wrong place but then he found her, crouched in a sodden, shivering huddle, trying to shield Ellis from the rain. Their mud-streaked faces looked spooky in the torchlight. She had been trying to dig more earth away from Ellis but his leg was still stuck.

"Matt!" Jem's voice sounded as though she was crying but her face was so wet with rain he couldn't be sure.

"It'll be OK now," he reassured her. Then Dad took over. He and Harry dug carefully all around Ellis' leg while Matt and Jem held torches. In no time there seemed to be lots of people and lights and Ellis was being lifted out of the mud and wrapped up like a parcel and carried off by some people with fluorescent stripes on their clothes. Then Matt and Jem were tottering back across the Acre. There were blue flashing lights down on the road and people talking, asking questions, giving instructions. Suddenly Matt felt very, *very* tired...

Wrapped in a blanket, warm and clean after a hot bath, Matt sat surrounded by the rest of the family and told the whole story, from the beginning. Only Mum and Dad asked questions. Stuart and Harry seemed to be stunned into silence and didn't interrupt at all.

"If I'd told you sooner, Ellis wouldn't have had the accident and he wouldn't be in hospital," Matt finished with a wobble in his voice.

"You did what you thought was right," said Mum, hugging him. "You were trying to be a good friend to Ellis."

"And he's only gone to hospital to be checked over," said Dad. "He had a bit of a shock and got very wet, that's all. His dad phoned while you were in the bath; Ellis is fine and he'll be home in the morning."

Matt sagged with relief.

"Fancy you kids thinking up something like that!" said Stuart.

"It wasn't really our idea," said Matt, wanting to be fair. "Harry told me about the bloke who lived in a tunnel and stopped the road being built—"

"Harry, *honestly*! Why don't you *think* before

you speak!" Mum exploded. Harry shrugged and grinned.

"Cool it, Mum! How was I to know little bruv and his friends would copy the idea?"

"This isn't a joke, Harry!" said Dad sternly. "What they did was *very* dangerous; there could have been a serious accident!"

"Yes, Harry, you complete and utter muppet!" Stuart groaned.

Slowly things were returning to normal as Stuart and Harry started to argue and Dad tried to talk over them and the phone rang again. Matt yawned. Now that he knew Ellis was going to be all right he felt warm and relaxed.

"It's a pity the tunnel didn't work," he said to Mum later, as he climbed into bed.

"How do you know it hasn't worked?" she asked.

"Ellis was going to phone the paper. He thought if the paper wrote about what he was doing then lots more people would know about what's happening to the Acre."

Mum smiled. "Don't worry; your hard work won't be wasted. I've a feeling lots of people are going to know what you three did!"

Matt lay listening to the sound of the rain still pattering on the window. The too-tight elastic seemed to have disappeared from his insides and he realised he wasn't worrying any more. He was almost asleep when he remembered something.

Thanks, God. Thanks for keeping Ellis and Jem safe. Thanks for helping me know what to do... and that Mum and Dad weren't cross... thanks for

Stuart and Harry, too... they're not bad, really...
still wish we could save the Acre... don't know
what'll happen now... you do, though... mmm...
goodnight, God...

Chapter Fifteen

"Move closer together. That's right. Big smile now!" The camera clicked again and again and Matt's face felt stiff with smiling. Jem was really enjoying herself. Dressed in her brightest clothes, she beamed radiantly, but Ellis could still only manage his almost-smile. Matt knew he was happy, though; Ellis just wasn't the sort of person who showed people what he was feeling. But if you were his friends, you knew.

The three of them were standing holding spades, near the remains of the tunnel, while the photographer from the local paper took pictures. It was two days since Ellis had been dug out of the mud. They had all had the following day off school because they were so tired, and their parents had done some very serious talking. All of them were impressed by what their children had been trying to do but they made them promise to never, *ever* do anything as dangerous as that again.

Now it was Saturday. The reporter from the paper had asked if she could interview them so they had come, with their parents, to show her where they had built their tunnel. It didn't feel like the same place, now that the sun was shining and the flood had nearly gone, but Matt shivered a bit as he looked at the heap of earth that had slipped down the bank and nearly buried Ellis.

"So, you decided to dig a tunnel here to stop the new houses being built on Shelley's Acre," said the reporter. All three of them nodded.

"This place must be very important to you to make you want to go to all that trouble." They nodded again.

"It's important to lots of people, not just us," Jem added.

"Didn't you think it was a bit dangerous to try and live in the tunnel?" the reporter turned to Ellis.

"No... er, a bit. But I had to do *something*!" Ellis replied firmly.

"You're a brave boy!" she said, smiling. Ellis shrugged.

"Couldn't have done it without my friends," he said. Matt and Jem grinned at him.

"Well, this is going to make a fantastic story!" the reporter continued, looking towards the group of parents who were chatting together. "Your children are going to make the headlines next week. Don't forget to buy lots of copies!"

Then she snapped her notebook shut and followed the photographer back to their car on the road.

"Everyone's coming back to our place for coffee," Mum called over to Matt, then she and Jem's mum and the Palmers began to walk away from the bike track.

"Coming?" asked Dad.

"Can we stay for a bit?" said Matt. "We want to see if we can find a few things we lost." Mr Cross, the farmer, had put up a fence around the area where the tunnel had been to stop people using the bike track. They'd had to climb over it for the photos, but they probably wouldn't be allowed back again after this.

"Hmm, don't know how easy that'll be," Dad replied. "What have you lost?"

Matt looked uncomfortable. "I um, I sort of borrowed a bucket and the picnic groundsheet," he mumbled.

"My school bag," said Ellis. "And Dad's mobile phone," he added quietly.

"Well, we can try, can't we?" Dad said as he took one of the spades.

Dad, Matt and Ellis dug in the loose earth where the tunnel doorway had been and Jem searched around the long grass and bushes nearby.

"Ah-ha!" shouted Dad. "This could be our groundsheet!" He started to pull at the corner of a bit of green plastic.

"Yuk! It'll need washing!" said Jem when they had hauled it out.

Soon after that they found the squashed remains of the bucket.

"Still no phone and school bag, though," sighed Matt.

"School bag's too far in," said Ellis. "Left it in the cave."

"Well, we certainly won't be able to dig right back there this morning," Dad decided, as he drove his spade into the earth one last time.

Clunk!

"What's that?" All four of them stared at the ground where the spade stuck out. Dad carefully pulled it out and scraped the earth away.

"Huh! It's that old dustbin lid!" Matt grunted.

"Are you sure that's what it is?" asked Dad, sticking the end of the spade under it and levering it out of the mud.

"Yes, we used it for a door, till Ellis made his super-fantastical drawbridge," Jem explained. Dad wasn't listening; he was looking at it closely. He scraped some of the dirt off it with his fingernails and then rubbed the patch with his sleeve.

"Where did you find this?" he asked. Matt pointed.

"We dug it up near there, when we first started the tunnel. Why?"

"I think this may be a bit more important than a dustbin lid," said Dad, looking excited. They crowded round and he pointed to where he'd started to clean. Instead of rusty grey iron they saw a patch of patterned metal that definitely wasn't the colour of a dustbin lid.

"What is it?" asked Jem, getting excited too.

"I'm not sure," Dad admitted. "But it may be special, so we're not leaving it here. Come on; time we went home!"

At home the sitting room filled with noise as Dad showed everyone what they'd dug up.

"What is it?"

"Oh, *please*! Don't put it on there; it's *filthy*!"

"Where did you find it?"

"No, Harry, it's *not* a giant frisbee!"

"What's it made of?"

"Who does it belong to?"

Dad and Mr Palmer took it off to the kitchen to clean it and Mum began offering more coffee. Matt, Jem and Ellis settled down round one end of the sofa with a plate of flapjacks.

"You OK now?" Matt asked Ellis. He shrugged and almost-smiled.

"Yup."

"It was *so* exciting!" said Jem, licking her fingers and reaching for another flapjack. "Scary too, though," she admitted.

Matt nodded as he remembered Ellis and Jem with their faces covered in mud, staring at him in the dark. "Pity it all went wrong," he sighed.

"Who says?" said Ellis. "Built the tunnel, didn't we? Newspaper people came. Lots of people will know about the Acre, won't they?"

Matt grinned as he realised what Ellis meant. "Yes, I s'pose it's worked... sort of."

"Mm, you nearly got buried for ever, Ellis," said Jem. "But you're safe and now the newspaper can tell everybody what happened and why we did it. I can't wait!"

"Coming back to school on Monday?" Matt asked Ellis.

"Yup."

"The project!" gasped Matt, staring at the others in horror. "We should be finished and we've hardly done anything for *ages*!"

"Don't panic!" Jem said calmly. "You and I have nearly finished ours, Matt," she reminded him. "And I bet Ellis gets more time, because of... you know... what Joey did."

Ellis didn't seem bothered. "Got it all saved," he said. "Just need to print it."

"I'll do the pictures again for you," Jem offered.

"Don't need to. Scanned 'em. Won't take long. No problem." He looked cheerful. Well, as cheerful as someone like Ellis ever looks.

"Phew!" Matt relaxed again and took another flapjack.

"Anyone want to come to town?" Dad stuck his head round the door. "I've just phoned the local history society and they say we can take our dustbin lid down to their office in the library. They'll contact English Heritage for us and then we can get an expert to look at it."

Chapter Sixteen

"That isn't me; it *can't* be!" Jem giggled.

It was Wednesday morning and Matt, Jem and Ellis were standing at the corner of Rickyard Close, looking at their photo in the local paper. Matt had gone early to the newsagent to get a copy of the paper because they badly wanted to see what the reporter had written. They were meant to be on their way to school but they'd forgotten the time.

After two days back at school, things were returning to normal again. It had been a relief to go back and do ordinary things after all the excitement of the past week. Matt was almost enjoying doing things like French tests and geometry. Almost. Ellis had quite a lot of work to catch up on in all his subjects, as well as the history project. Matt and Jem were worried about this, too, but they found that a lot of other people hadn't finished their projects either. Now, today, everyone would know the real reason why Ellis had been off school last week. All three friends were excited, but only Jem showed it. She was usually quite calm, but this morning she kept hugging the others and saying, "Exciting-soooo-exciting!"

"Pity about the photo," Ellis sighed, trying to avoid another hug.

"Yes, pity," Matt agreed gloomily.

"You can see it's us, though, can't you?" said Jem, a bit doubtful.

It really was a huge picture; nearly half the front page.

What if everyone on the planet sees this awful picture of us, and the plan still doesn't work? We'll be dying of embarrassment for nothing!

"'Local Hero buried alive!'" Jem read the headline. "Wow, dramatic or what!"

"Says we were trying to save Shelley's Acre; that's the important bit," Ellis said quietly. He had been reading the small print carefully. The article was quite long but the reporter had told their story well, even if they didn't like some of the things she'd written.

"'Pint-sized environmentalists... hair-raising tunnelling technique'. Huh, cheek!" Ellis grunted. "Tunnel would've been OK if it hadn't rained so much." He folded up the paper and they walked on to school.

Before they had even reached the gate people were coming up or calling out to them as they passed. Anyone who hadn't read the newspaper yet got told about the article by those who had. Soon it seemed as though the whole school knew.

At registration Mrs Brown mentioned it and in their history lesson there was so much excitement fizzing around the room that Mr Hicks got Ellis, Matt and Jem to sit at the front and answer questions from the rest of the class.

"We don't know if it'll do any good, though," Matt said at the end.

"You'd be surprised what ordinary people can achieve," said Mr Hicks. "If you're determined and organised and you can get enough of the population to support you, things happen! But don't go home and tell your parents I said you've all got to start digging tunnels!"

"Why didn't you eat your sandwiches?" asked Mum when Matt got home.

"I didn't need them," he explained. "People kept buying us crisps and chocolate at lunch time; I thought I was going to burst!"

"It must be nice to be famous!" Mum laughed.

"Ellis is the important one, really. He did the dangerous bit."

"Yes, he's certainly very determined," Mum agreed. "I wonder what made him do it?"

"I think it was because people were giving him a hard time about living in one of the new houses."

"You mean people like that boy Joey?"

"Yes. I think Ellis wanted to do something to show he belonged here; that he was one of us."

"Well, everyone was talking about the newspaper article at work today," said Mum. "A lot more people know what's happening to Shelley's Acre now, so part of your plan has worked. And, there's something else..." She paused, looking very pleased. "Mr Neil from the local history society came to see me in the library this morning. He brought an archaeologist with him from English Heritage."

Matt looked blank.

"A person who finds out about the history of a place by digging in the ground and studying the things they find," Mum explained. "She says your dustbin lid could be very important and very valuable indeed."

"Is it old?" said Matt.

"*Extremely* old!" Mum smiled. "She thinks it's almost definitely Roman!"

"What!" Matt stared at her. "You mean, really *Roman*? Older than the church? Older than the old tree, and all that?"

Mum nodded.

"Phew!" Matt sat down to think.

"They've been in touch with Mr Cross and they're going to move his little wire fence round the tunnel and build a proper, high fence. Once word gets around about what you found, people will want to go and look and some of them may cause damage or even try to steal things. The area will be guarded until the archaeologist and her team can dig to see if there's anything else buried there."

Matt's brain was churning with jumbled thoughts. He grabbed hold of one and held on to it. "So, they won't be able to start building yet?"

"No, I don't think they will," Mum said.

Matt looked at her and grinned. "Brilliant! Mega-mega brilliant!"

Later, after tea, Matt was round at Jem's house, working on their project. The living room floor was covered in big sheets of cardboard and glue and scissors. They were trying to arrange bits of writing, photos and pictures to make their display. Jem had calmed down now but Matt made sure he was too far away to be hugged when he told her Mum's news. She didn't say anything for a moment but just sat there, twirling the end of her braid and staring into space.

"Wow!" she whispered at last. "That is *so* fantastic! God *does* answer prayers."

"Have you been talking to God, too?" asked Matt. Jem nodded.

"At Club Baz and Steffi keep telling us that we can talk to God about things, don't they? Well, I've been telling him about the Acre and our plan and asking if he could do something about it for us... and it looks like he has!"

"Yes," Matt agreed.

"I was waiting and waiting and thinking maybe it wasn't important enough for God to be interested in, because nothing seemed to be happening," said Jem. "But now I think he was waiting to see if we were really serious. When we started to do something, he helped us!"

"I think he could have done it all without us, though," said Matt. "But maybe he likes us to work with him."

"Mm," Jem nodded. "It's the same as us just sitting here, waiting for him to finish our project for us. Nothing would happen, would it?"

"No, because he knows we can do that ourselves!"

"Yes, but something like saving Shelley's Acre is really hard, so he waited until we got started and now he's beginning to do things!"

"But they may still build the houses, when the archeologist finishes digging," Matt reminded her. Jem shrugged.

"Maybe, but I'm going to keep praying! Now, where are we going to stick this picture?"

They went on working and gradually the display began to take shape. As he worked, Matt thought about what had happened since he had started talking to God again.

Last week I was worrying about the Acre but I was worried about Ellis and me, too... It was really hard to know how to be a good friend to Ellis... At school, when Joey and his lot were being pains I always knew, really, what I had to do... I was just a bit chicken. But when Ellis started skipping school and we had our plan, well, I didn't know what was right... God knew what was going on, though... and I think he knows all about Ellis and his family, too. When Ellis was in danger, I just knew what to do... and now, even though Ellis knows I told Mum and Dad, he's still my friend... I'm glad I let God help me!

"Sorry, kids," said Jem's mum. "I've got some friends coming round soon; you'll have to clear all this up." She looked at what they'd done. "That's really good; better than some of the work my A level students are doing!"

She went to find a folder to store the finished sheets in, while Jem and Matt tidied up.

"Have you noticed – Ellis is different?" Jem said.

Matt stopped collecting felt-tip pens. "Is he?"

"Yes, he's not grumpy any more. I think he's happier."

"Maybe he feels he belongs here now. I mean, after what he did in the tunnel, everyone's being very friendly to him."

"Almost everyone!" Jem said.

"Joey, you mean?"

Jem nodded. "He's been keeping out of the way since Ellis came back."

"Probably planning something!"

"I hope not!" Jem made a face. "We'd better stick close to Ellis, in case he still needs us... that's if he wants us."

"I'm sure he knows we're really his mates now," Matt said. "We kept the secret till we had to get help. And you stayed with him in the rain when the tunnel collapsed."

"Someone had to," said Jem. "I'm glad I did... but I was *really* scared!" She shivered. "I talked to God a lot then," she remembered. "I kept asking him to keep Ellis safe and to help you find your way home, quickly. I was scared but I knew God was there with us."

"I was scared, too," Matt admitted. "I wonder if Ellis knows that God was looking after us all?"

"We could tell everyone at Club this week, at Sharing Time," Jem suggested. "It could be a really good thing for the 'Thank you' bit, like when Steffi told us how God helped her when her mum was ill."

"Yes, and we could ask Ellis to come," added Matt. "I think he'd like Club now."

Chapter Seventeen

"Can I borrow a fine-liner?" Matt shouted from the doorway of his brother's room. Stuart was hunched over his desk, scribbling furiously, with books and papers scattered around him and music pounding out of his stereo. He reduced the volume.

"OK, but I want it back. And *not* covered in mud, like my torch was!"

Matt grabbed the pen and scuttled back to his own room where he was trying to draw extra neat triangles for geometry homework.

"Hey, wassup, Indiana? How's Tunnel Man?" Harry poked his head round the door. Matt was getting a bit sick of his new name, though Tunnel Man fitted Ellis all right. Ever since the archaeologist had confirmed that the dustbin lid was really a Roman platter, and her team had begun work at the bike track, Harry had been calling him Indiana Jones. He hummed the theme tune whenever he saw him.

"Go away, Harry," Matt muttered. Harry ignored this and sprawled across his bed.

"Just been over to the dig, on my way home from work," he announced. "Saw that professor woman; the archaeologist. She was *well* excited!"

Matt stopped working. "Why?"

"They've found some more stuff!"

Matt was really interested now. "How come she told you?"

"She recognised me because I went with Dad when he took your dustbin lid to the library, remember?" Matt nodded.

"Actually," he continued, looking smug, "she said I could take you and the others over and we could have a look... now! Our own private visit: no one else is allowed yet. Coming?"

Matt leapt off his chair and dashed to the phone while Harry lay, grinning at the ceiling and humming.

Ten minutes later Harry and Matt, Jem and Ellis were running across Shelley's Acre towards the bike track, which was now surrounded by a high fence with 'keep out' and 'danger' notices on it.

It was evening and work had finished. People were packing up but Professor Morris was in the hut that had been brought as an office and a shelter for the people on guard duty at night. When they arrived she closed her laptop and came to unlock the gate.

"Wow, what's happened to the bike track?" Jem gasped as soon as they were through the fence. The whole of the highest hump had moved! A mini digger stood beside a new heap of freshly dug soil and, where the hump with the tunnel had been, a large tarpaulin was spread out.

"Come and see what we've found!" said Professor Morris with an excited smile. "When we'd identified your find as Roman I felt certain it was worth digging here," she said. "As you probably know, there was a small Roman settlement here from about AD 150."

"So, did the platter belong to a house near here?" asked Jem.

"I wasn't sure," the professor continued. "It was possible that it had been buried in the field at some other time in history, maybe by someone who had stolen it somewhere else and wanted to hide it, or by someone who wanted to keep it safe from enemy invaders, but we had to check out the Roman connection properly." They followed her down towards the tarpaulin. "I'm so glad we did," she continued. "Because we've found this!"

She pulled up a corner of the tarpaulin and they stared down into a hole. First, all they saw was dark, lumpy soil and then, beyond this, lay a smoother, level surface. It was smeared with mud but one little patch had been cleaned and there they could clearly see a pattern. Tiny red, black and white square stones were arranged neatly into some lines and a swirly shape.

"Hey, is that a mosaic?" said Harry.

The professor nodded. "We've only cleared a little bit so far and there could be a lot more but, yes, it looks very much as though we've found the remains of a Roman mosaic floor."

"A real mosaic?" asked Matt. He couldn't believe it. He'd seen pictures in books but never the real thing. "What's it doing here in a field?"

"Remember, the history books said that there would have been farms around here when the Romans lived here," said Harry. "In my project..." He was starting to take over the conversation, as usual.

"So, a Roman villa, yeah?" Ellis interrupted.

"Yes, I think we can safely say that," the

professor agreed. "It was probably one of several in the area, with large farms attached. They would have provided food for the local settlement and for the soldiers in the garrison down on the coast. Other remains have been found in this part of the country in the past but nothing of this quality. It could be over eighteen hundred years old!"

"It's been here under the ground all that time and we've been riding our bikes over it!" said Matt.

"We don't know why it was under these mounds of earth," said the professor. "But it meant that it was kept safe until now."

"Fan*tas*tic!" Jem whispered, staring at the small patch of intricate pattern. "All those tiny stones... it's so beautiful... oh, *wow*! Wait till Mum hears about this!"

"You're some of the first people to see this for perhaps more than a thousand years," said the professor. "And I'm very glad you are because, if it hadn't been for the heavy rain softening the earth and your tunnel collapsing, we might not have found it until it was too late."

"Why?" asked Matt.

"Well, it might just have stayed hidden under your bike track or, as this land has been sold for housing, we might have been called in to look at this beautiful floor after it had been badly scrunched up by a bulldozer!"

Matt winced at the thought.

"What next?" Ellis wanted to know.

"We'll have to uncover everything important here."

"What about the houses, though?" Matt asked, anxiously.

"Nothing can happen until we've finished, but we must work quickly because the new owners of the land are waiting to know what'll happen. People who are more important than me will come and look and they'll decide."

"No houses yet, though?" Ellis asked. The professor smiled.

"No houses yet. Definitely!"

"Yesss!" shouted Matt.

"Oooooh!" Jem needed to hug someone and Harry was the nearest.

"Hey, nice work, Tunnel Man!" he said, hugging her back and grinning at Ellis. Then he looked at his watch. "Time to go Indiana; I need food!" They turned towards the gate.

"Before you go," said the professor. "Do these things belong to you?" She went to the shed and brought back a very tattered school bag. "Someone spotted them while we were digging but I don't know if this will ever work again!" she laughed as she held out the mobile phone. Ellis gave his almost-smile as he took them.

When they got home Matt became invisible again because, of course, Harry had a lot to say about where they had been. He was really enjoying knowing something before Stuart did. Matt didn't mind. He sat in a happy dream, hardly listening, as questions and answers pinged to and fro around him.

No building yet. So, maybe the plan's still working, even though it's a bit different from when we started. We thought when the tunnel collapsed everything was spoilt but we still got our story in the paper and now... wow! There's still a chance that we can save the Acre after all. God, you're excellent!

Chapter Eighteen

"Hey, help me shift this table, can you?"

"Who's got the staple gun?"

"No, that's too high... down a bit..."

Mr Hicks had decided to use the whole of the history lesson to set out the finished projects in the school hall, ready for the parents' evening later in the week. Folders and models were being spread neatly on tables, and maps, pictures and photos displayed on walls and screens. In one corner Matt was wrestling with a roll of sticky tape while Jem was placing her model of St Ann's church in front of their writing and photos. Ellis was working next to them. He'd managed to redo the parts of his project that were ruined, and Jem had helped him make a huge collage of the old yew tree from strips of green paper and bark rubbings from the actual tree. It had little labels on it to say what would have been happening in history at different stages of its life.

"Ah, excellent, *excellent*!" beamed Mr Hicks as he passed. "When you've finished here would you come and help us with the extra display, please?"

A lot had happened since the mosaic had been discovered. Professor Morris and her team had worked hard and uncovered a complete floor and foundations for some walls. They had also found a very interesting Roman rubbish dump, full of chicken bones and pieces of broken pottery. There had been nothing else as grand as the dustbin lid platter, though. All these things were taken away to be cleaned and examined carefully. Matt, Jem and Ellis had been to the dig to have their photos taken for the paper *again* and then the whole history class had gone to see the floor for themselves. This was a real privilege because the general public wasn't allowed in until all work was finished. It was important to work as fast as possible because Smart Homes were getting impatient.

After the visit Mr Hicks decided to organise a last-minute display for the parents to see. "I feel as if this discovery belongs to us," he said, "seeing as three members of our class were so involved!" He had taken lots of photos and a few people who'd finished their projects had volunteered to help him find more information about life in the area in Roman times. So now there was an extra display called 'The Shelley's Acre Mosaic'.

Matt finally unstuck himself and he and Ellis joined the group who were already working on the mosaic display. Someone turned round as they arrived.

"Hey, Tunnel Man!" It was Joey, grinning and waving the staple gun. Matt froze and looked at Ellis.

Oh no, The Mouth! It would be! He's been mighty quiet for ages. What's he going to do now?

Ellis just looked at Joey and nodded.

"Pretty famous now, aren't ya? Pictures in the paper; doing all that stuff," said Joey.

Ellis shrugged. "Needed to do something about

the Acre."

"Did ya? *Really*? Even though you're the new kid?" Joey was really staring at Ellis now. Matt got ready to move in and do his Guardian Angel act again.

I expect he's jealous of Ellis. He's never been famous for anything, except being a Grade A pain in the neck. He can't stand it that everyone's talking to Ellis and he's not getting any attention. I wish he'd put that staple gun down!

Joey was smiling his usual 'I'm-bigger-and-badder-than-you-and-I've-just-thought-of-something-really-nasty-to-do-to-you' smile and Matt's stomach was tying itself in a knot when Tim, one of Joey's gang, pushed to the front of the group.

"Put it there, mate!" he said, holding out his hand for Ellis to shake. "That was great, what you did in that tunnel. Is it true you got buried alive?"

"Nearly," Ellis replied. "Matt and Jem rescued me."

"Nice work!" said Tim, including Matt in his smile. "You and the hippie. That was good."

"Right lads, let's get this finished!" Mr Hicks bustled back to join them.

"Sir," said Tim, "Ellis is a hero, isn't he?"

"Well, one way or another, he and Matt and Jem have managed to get plenty of publicity for Shelley's Acre," Mr Hicks agreed. "And finding the mosaic was a wonderful bonus. Yes, I think all three of them are heroes of a kind!"

"There!" said Tim, glaring round at Joey and the rest. "Anyone wanna argue about it?"

No, nobody did.

On the way home from school that afternoon, Matt and Jem stopped with Ellis at the end of Rickyard Close.

"That was nice, what Mr Hicks said about us," said Jem.

"Hey, and what about Tim, eh?" Matt shook his head in amazement.

"He's OK," said Ellis. "Cares about the Acre."

"Wonder when they'll decide what's going to happen to the Acre?" said Matt.

"Maybe they'll say something at the meeting tomorrow," said Jem. "Are you going?"

"Yes, we all are; even Harry!" Matt remembered something and turned to Ellis. "Tonight's Club, are you coming again?"

Ellis had come to Club the previous week and seemed to enjoy it in his quiet way. At Sharing Time Matt and Jem had talked about how God had helped them when Ellis had the accident. Not all the details of course, because they didn't want to embarrass him. He didn't seem to mind but he hadn't said anything afterwards.

"Yeah," said Ellis. "It was good." He paused. "So, God was looking after us?" he said suddenly. "You believe that?"

Matt and Jem both nodded. He turned into Rickyard Close. "OK. See ya tonight." And he walked off up the path.

The Community Centre was crammed for the public meeting the following evening. Matt and his family were late because Dad's train had been delayed. They squeezed into some empty seats at the very back, just as someone on the platform stood up.

"Mrs Brewer, our local councillor," Dad whispered.

Matt listened, but didn't really understand what she was saying. He looked at the platform and recognised someone sitting there.

"...and I'd like to invite Professor Morris, the archaeologist from English Heritage, to give us her report," said Councillor Brewer.

Professor Morris didn't speak for long, but what she said started an excited hum of voices around the hall.

"What? *What*?" Matt asked Dad. He wasn't sure why people were so excited.

"English Heritage want more time to excavate the area properly and they want it to become a permanent site of historic interest," Dad explained loudly over the babble of voices.

"Will that mean they won't build houses there?" asked Matt. Dad nodded.

"Not yet... well not where the bike track is, anyway."

"But what about—"

"Shhhh!" Someone else was being introduced by Councillor Brewer.

"—the spokesperson for Smart Homes," she said and sat down.

Matt tried to listen but he felt hot and squashed and the man was talking about 'greenfield sites' and 'viable business propositions'. As the man from Smart Homes finished, the hum of voices began again, louder than ever. Councillor Brewer was shaking his hand and then she turned and hugged Professor Morris. There was an explosion of clapping and cheers.

"What?" Matt was confused.

"Smart Homes have decided not to build on Shelley's Acre," Dad explained. "They're building down by the station after all!"

"We've won!" shouted Stuart.

Harry stopped stamping and whistling and turned to Matt. "Well done, little bruv; you and your mates have saved Shelley's Acre!"

Much later that evening the whole family were sitting around the kitchen with bedtime drinks, though no one felt ready for bed yet. There had been so much noise and excitement at the hall that Matt still didn't really understand what had happened.

"Smart Homes realised that finding the mosaic was very important," Dad said.

"They were as excited as everyone else about that," said Mum. "The trouble was, if they couldn't build where the mosaic was, there wasn't enough room left to build all the houses they wanted to."

"So they've done a deal with the council," Dad went on. "They will give Shelley's Acre to the council to use as a recreation area, in exchange for the old swimming pool site by the station."

"So we'll still be able to use the Acre?" said Matt.

"Not the bit where the mosaic is; that'll be turned into a site of historic interest for people to visit," Stuart reminded them.

"Like Stonehenge?" Harry joined in.

"They'll need to make a car park, I suppose," said Mum. "I hope there'll still be some Acre left for us to use."

"There'll be plenty of space," said Dad. "That field is far larger than just an acre."

"Hectare," Stuart corrected him.

"But we'll still be able to use it?" Matt asked again, loudly. He had the feeling he was starting to become invisible again.

"That's what Councillor Brewer said," Mum reassured him.

"Good," Matt murmured to himself.

"Hey, there could be a shop and we could sell Shelley's Acre mosaic T-shirts!" Harry was starting to get carried away. "Or... or Gino could make special Mosaic pizzas and I could sell them and—" Stuart rolled his eyes.

"Have you been taking Stupid Idea lessons again?"

Stuart and Harry had taken over as usual. Matt didn't care. He caught Mum's eye and she smiled at him. Then she looked at her watch. "Bed!" she said firmly, nodding towards the door.

Chapter Nineteen

Matt and Jem sat against the trunk of the old yew tree in the summer sunshine.

They came here a lot now that they couldn't use the bike track. Shelley's Acre had shrunk a bit, with one corner turned into a visitor centre for people coming to see the mosaic. They could still use the footpath as a shortcut to school, and there was plenty of room to play football, but they needed somewhere special to meet until everything had settled down and they had got used to the changes.

"I'm glad there aren't any houses on the Acre but I miss the bike track," said Matt.

"When they've finished the visitor centre maybe we could make another one," Jem suggested. She was carefully making a daisy chain.

"It'll be open soon," she added. "Before the summer holidays."

A few days earlier they had all been invited, with their families, to the almost finished site. The corner where the bike track had been was now transformed. Inside the high fence the land was flat and a building had been put up to protect the mosaic. There was a room for displays and information and a small shop selling things like postcards and books, but no pizzas.

The mosaic was clean now and surrounded by a

low rail so you could lean over and look, without falling into the hole. The border looked like twined rope and in the centre was a big diamond shape with a circle of little fish inside.

"It's such a beautiful pattern," said Matt's mum as they stood looking down on it. The patterns of tiny coloured squares gleamed under the spotlights.

"Must've been dead fiddly to make!" said Matt. He hated doing things like jigsaw puzzles.

"Where's our dustbin lid?" asked Jem.

"I'm afraid that will have to stay in the museum," explained Professor Morris. "It's very valuable. You must come and see it soon." Then she showed them some photos of it.

"Oh, it's shiny!" laughed Jem. All the mud had been cleaned off and now the pattern around the edge stood out clearly. It was leaves and curly stems, all twisted together.

"Yes, it's silver," Professor Morris explained. "It's cleaned up beautifully, considering it'd been underground for so long."

"Looks great," said Matt's dad.

"Just as well," grunted Ellis. "Made a useless front door!" He still mostly talked in words rather than proper sentences, but he could do real smiles now. He came to Club most weeks and he seemed happy at school. The best bit was Joey never had a go at him now and no one called him New Kid any more.

"Remember hiding in here when Joey and the gang were chasing us?" said Matt, looking at the hole in the tree trunk.

Jem nodded. "He's been very quiet since Tim and

126

some of the others started to be friendly." She joined the daisy chain into a circle. Matt thought for a bit.

"The tree's a thousand years old, which is 'half-way back to Jesus', like Mum said. We thought *that* was old!" He laughed. "But when the tree was planted and some of the old bits of the church were being built, the mosaic was already over *eight hundred* years old!"

"Almost *all* the way back to Jesus!" said Jem. "*Two* millenniums!"

"Millennia."

"You're starting to sound like your brother!"

"*Loads* of people have lived here," said Matt. "Like the Roman ones who came and built the villa."

"...the one with the clever fingers who made the mosaic," Jem added.

"...ones who built the church."

"...planted this tree!"

"Wonder what they'd think if they were here now?"

"If it was me, I'd be proud that my mosaic still looked so good!" said Jem.

"And I'd be amazed how big my tree was!" Matt thought again. "They might be sad to see how different some things are, though."

"Maybe," said Jem, hanging the daisy chain round her neck. "But I think they'd be pleased there's still a church here and that people still believe in Jesus."

"It's tea-time," said Matt, looking at his watch.

"Going to Club tonight?"

"Yes, Mum's taking."

"See you later."

Mum smiled as he came into the kitchen. "Tea's nearly ready; can you set the table?" Then she started to peer at the instructions on a packet of pasta. Matt fetched the mats and cutlery.

It's funny how things work out. A while ago we thought we would never be able to use the Acre again and I was worried that I'd never be brave enough help Ellis. They were big problems, like Gideon's huge army of enemies! But God showed me how to handle them. Talking to him really helped.

"Yo, Mother-Dear!" Harry bounced through the door and flung himself down on the nearest chair. "I've seen another a-maaazing guitar—"

"Harry, did you borrow this T-shirt?" Stuart stormed into the kitchen, waving something crumpled and dirty.

Matt sighed. Life was definitely back to normal now. As long as Harry and Stuart were around, there would be times when he would feel as though he was invisible. But he didn't mind because he knew he wasn't, really. Most important of all, even when other people didn't notice him and no one seemed to be listening, he knew God was there. God could see him and he was happy to listen to Matt *any* time.